The Final Hour

The
Final Hour

Naguib Mahfouz

)(

Translated by
Roger Allen

The American University in Cairo Press
Cairo   New York

First published in 2010 by
The American University in Cairo Press
113 Sharia Kasr el Aini, Cairo, Egypt
420 Fifth Avenue, New York, NY 10018
www.aucpress.com

Dar el Kutub No. 2264/10
ISBN 978 977 416 388 3

Dar el Kutub Cataloging-in-Publication Data

Mahfouz, Naguib 1911–2006
        The Final Hour /Naguib Mahfouz; translated by Roger Allen.—
Cairo: The American University in Cairo Press, 2010
        p.   cm.
        ISBN 978 977 416 388 3
        1. Arabic fiction   I. Allen, Roger (trans.) II. Title
        892.73

1 2 3 4 5 6 7 8   15 14 13 12 11 10

Designed by Andrea el-Akshar
Printed in Egypt

Whenever she felt nostalgic, she would always go back and look at the commemorative photograph. The green walls of the living room were decorated with three gilt-edged frames: the middle one was a calligraphic version of the Basmallah; to the right, her old primary school certificate; and to the left a photograph commemorating their day trip. Over the years she had forgotten many things, but the occasion when that photograph had been taken way back in 1932 was one that she had never forgotten. On that day eternity had been granted to that particular moment in her family's history.

There she is, sitting happily on a rug laid out on the grass at the Qanatir Gardens. Hamid Burhan, head of the family, sits right in the middle; his legs are stretched out, and he looks a picture of health, handsome with his olive complexion and well-proportioned features. To his right is she herself, Saniya al-Mahdi, sitting cross-legged, her lap and legs covered with a wide shawl decorated with exquisite needlepoint detail. On his left sits Kawthar, the eldest child, looking suitably lovely and staring modestly at the camera. Next to her (and in family order as well) comes Muhammad, with exactly the same features as his father; followed by Munira, whose beauty is far more spectacular, as is her expression. At the time the father is fifty and the mother forty, and the children are adolescents. Everyone is smiling, their expressions showing how happy they are about the trip and the peace and quiet of the surroundings. In front of them are bottles of fizzy water, paper plates piled high with sandwiches, bananas, and oranges. Behind them looms a grassy slope and a smattering of trees. Beyond all that, you can see the minarets of the Qanatir district and groups of people milling around. The entire photograph invokes a sense of utter sweetness, with no sign of the times even slightly evident.

Outside the context of that photograph, however, time—needless to say—has not stood still. One of its dictates has decreed that, of the members of the family, only the mistress, Saniya al-Mahdi, and her eldest daughter, Kawthar, are still living in the house. It is a big house made up of a single story that rises out of the ground in five levels, with a garden on the south side. The entire plot consists of half a feddan. For at least one generation it flourished, but that was followed by several decades of decline and outright desertion. The sheer size of the house and its garden is one of the relics of the Helwan of old, far away from Cairo, but cheap, and a haven of peace and contemplation. To indulge in its mineral waters, saltpeter baths, and Japanese Garden was a cure package for nervous tensions, aching joints, and souls in torment, let alone people in search of a patch of quiet seclusion. On Ibn Hawqal Street all the houses looked the same; all, that is, except the one opposite the family home that had been sold during the Second World War so that a new one could be built. The al-Mahdi house was noted for its green paint—that being the color used in most of the rooms with their high ceilings. The same color had been used for the lounge, a reflection of its mistress's predilections and the continuing devotion she felt for the house, that in itself being a source of problems for her children and grandchildren that they had so far been unable to resolve.

The person who originally built the house was her father, Abdallah al-Mahdi, who toward the end of his long life had been a reasonably wealthy farmer. When rheumatism laid him low, he was advised to take up residence in Helwan, which was then a health center known for the dryness of its climate. He sold some of his property and built the house, leaving the rest of the land to his son, al-Bakri, and moved to Helwan with his wife and only daughter, Saniya. He later distributed his property by mutual consent between his son and daughter, leaving the house to her. It had played a significant role in her life. When the matchmaker suggested to Hamid's mother that Saniya would be a suitable bride, she extolled the house to the skies; some of its features were certainly enough of an incentive when it came to making such an important choice in life. In addition to all that, Saniya was not bad looking and had managed to earn her primary school certificate. She was known to be intelligent; if her father had not insisted on keeping her secluded, she could certainly have completed her education. How saddened she had been by his decision; how many tears she had shed in protest! That was why, in spite of her duties as mistress of the house and mother, she still insisted on reading newspapers and magazines and broadening her perspective on things, to such an extent that she managed to achieve an unusual degree of intellectual maturity that she regularly relied on to bolster her spiritual instincts and remarkable aspirations. She may well have been the only woman on Ibn Hawqal Street who kept an account book for the family budget and who corresponded on a regular basis with her brother; all of which may have been motivated by a desire to express herself and show everyone that she could do so.

She clearly felt a deep affection for her husband, Hamid Burhan, something that went back many, many years. Yet deep down she felt that she was better than him when it came to both sheer intelligence and common sense; he had only obtained a

3

primary-school certificate, after which he had enrolled in the Telegraph School and graduated from it.

Added to which was the fact that the only member of his own family whom he knew was a single forefather; even then, all he knew was his name. By contrast, she knew a whole host of ancestors, although she would only refer to them briefly and on rare occasions. An exception was her grandfather on her father's side who had taken the major step of converting to Islam even though he was from a Coptic heritage of long standing.

"My past history's not all that serene!" she admitted to her husband, Hamid Burhan, one day.

Hamid Burhan resembled his wife in that he too loved showing off. His basic lifestyle was simple and modest, and yet he would make the most of his attainments. He would insist on proving his manliness, even though there was no way of avoiding the glaring reality that his wife was the huge house's real mistress and ran it with judicious care. When it came to the children's upbringing, she was always the one to use discretion and firm guidance, not to mention the obvious fact that she was the one who fostered the happy familial atmosphere that he had been able to enjoy for so long. Another example of his tendency to boast was the way he always insisted on describing his role in the one political event in his life in which he had participated, namely his advocacy of the government workers' strike during the very first days of the 1919 Revolution. Every time the opportunity presented itself, he used to retell every single detail, realizing full well that it was the only political act in his entire life. The only vestige that remained from those days long ago was a heartfelt devotion to the Wafd Party, a sentiment that only revealed itself in any practical way on the rare occasions when free elections between political parties were permitted.

In a number of ways he was an exemplary father, deeply devoted to his wife and children. Among men of his age he was a paragon of health and vigor, totally free of the illnesses that would plague the dispositions of minor bureaucrats such as himself. He neither drank nor smoked, and his eye never wandered. He would spend the evening with colleagues, in the reception room in wintertime, and on the veranda the rest of the year. Like him these colleagues were from Helwan. There was Gaafar Ibrahim, a retired inspector; Khalil al-Dars, house manager for Nuaman al-Rashidi, a local aristocrat; Hasan Alama, an architect; and Radi Abu al-Azm, a science teacher. They used to spend their nights chatting, playing backgammon, and discussing politics—the last being an activity where they all sang the same tune with Wafdist origins, no argument and no discussion. Hamid Burhan was known to be neat and tidy, some-one with the tolerant and relaxed approach to piety that was a hallmark of the family as a whole. God first gave the parents the joy and comfort of two children, Muhammad and Munira, both of whom pursued their educational careers with conspicuous success, especially Munira, who was notable for both her beauty and intelligence. But there was another daughter too, Kawthar. She proved to be far more problematic, showing no interest in school and making little progress. Instead she was by nature more inclined to religious devotions and household matters. When she failed the general certificate of secondary education two years running, she was forced to stay at home.

"These days, people don't want a woman who stays at home," was Saniya's comment to Hamid at the time.

Hamid was well aware that Kawthar was not particularly good-looking either, and that made him feel very sad. "There's always luck," he said. "It doesn't have rules!"

The family had its own social routine together; they all par-ticularly enjoyed going on day trips. One time it might be to the Japanese Garden, another to the Qanatir Park, still another to the Archaeology Museum. Even though there was a serious world crisis at the time, civil servants with fixed incomes in Egypt could still live a pleasant life in the shadow of recession and falling prices. The raging financial storm may have uprooted everything that was still standing, but below the grass there was refuge to be found in safe havens where they could at least be merry and sing songs. Hamid Burhan allowed his family to act as it wished, with no restraints, unbothered by gossip, and never inclined to social formalities. After all, behind him stood a woman who was an excellent nurturer of her children, a veritable model when it came to fulfilling her obligations and behaving in the most appropriate manner imaginable.

As the days went by, however, no one came forward to seek Kawthar's hand in marriage, she being, of course, the one child for whom marriage was the only goal. Every time she prayed, Saniya would stretch out her hands in supplication. Sometimes her whole face would light up in a smile.

"I had a dream," she would say, "and I think it's important!"

She used to ask Umm Sayyid to read her coffee grounds, and then listen carefully to her rosy prognostications which managed to make Hamid feel a bit more hopeful and push his worries aside for a while. He soon forgot such things as he started following the news about the demonstrations and street fights that accompanied the 1923 constitution and the initiatives aimed at forging a sense of national unity in order to confront the crisis. All the effort and bloodshed involved led to a totally unexpected result, the signing of the 1936 treaty. That night Hamid's euphoria made him seem almost drunk.

"Now," he told his companions triumphantly, "all the Wafd's efforts have been crowned with a clear victory!"

To be sure, different opinions on the subject were expressed by Radi Abu al-Azm, the science teacher. "The preacher of heresy doesn't have to be a heretic!" he muttered apologetically, that being an expression that both Muhammad and Munira had said earlier on the basis of something they heard at school and repeated. Even so it had little effect in this household. Saniya was as much a Wafdist as her husband, and so was Muhammad. Even Munira was considered to be one too, although not very enthusiastic about it. Kawthar on the other hand was only concerned about her stomach. That evening the Wafd dominated the conversation.

"How could they have been expecting any better result?" asked Gaafar Ibrahim.

"This treaty," Hasan Alama responded, "is the result of a bitter struggle between an imperialist tyrant on the one hand and a defenseless country on the other. In any case it's bound to be carefully monitored . . . ."

"Anyone who's not happy about it can march with his army against the enemy!"

"The time for cursing is at an end," said Khalil al-Dars, Nuaman al-Rashidi's house manager. "Now the Wafd can rule forever."

However it seemed that the time for cursing had no desire to come to an end. A new struggle now burst into the open between the Wafd and the new king. A fight over a campaign against poverty, ignorance, and disease suddenly became a more traditional conflict over the constitution and democratic rule. The Wafd was thrown out, and in came the minority parties who agreed to play a phony democratic role that provided shameless cover for an act of monarchical despotism.

The group of men stared at each other, their utter dismay fired by genuine anger. They had all hoped that the people would rise up in anger as they had before, but instead they had all preferred to give up their classic role on the stage and sit in the audience.

"How on earth did our luck turn so bad?" Hamid Burhan asked.

Saniya stole a glance at her daughter, Kawthar. "Yes indeed," she thought to herself, "as bad as yours, my daughter!"

All over the world the atmosphere darkened, and sparks started to fly. Before long, the sickly veil was thrown off and another World War started.

"Italy's in Libya already," several people said. "Just a stone's throw away!"

By this time Muhammad had enrolled in the Faculty of Law, and Munira was about to go to the Liberal Arts College. Kawthar, meanwhile, was still waiting. Like his father, Muhammad had been devastated by the Wafd's defeat and stories of infighting. One day he noticed a sign stuck to the bars of an apartment balcony on Saafan Street; in Persian script it said "The Muslim Brotherhood." A blend of sheer curiosity and concern led him to make his way into the apartment. Thereafter he used to go there once in a while and give his family reports about what had happened. This went on for a while, but eventually his father spoke to him, "That's enough. I'm not too happy about this situation . . . ."

The young man did his best to defend his point of view, but his father would not hear of it.

"You're a Wafdist," he told his son. "Any other group has to be a rival for the Wafd."

"But it's open to everyone," Muhammad insisted.

At that point in time, nothing about Muhammad changed except that he started adding religious texts to his reading list. Even so, Kawthar was still more devout than he was, although her meek expression conveyed a permanent feeling of profound sadness. What only added to the family's tensions was that a forty-five year old director-general with the railways came to ask for Munira's hand just as she was getting ready to go to university. As far as Hamid Burhan was concerned, the man's senior position certainly made him attractive but, like his wife, Saniya, he was still worried about Kawthar. Whatever the case, the matter had to be discussed with Munira.

"No, I won't agree!" she responded firmly, much to everyone's astonishment.

"It would be a good idea," Muhammad commented, "to give it some thought before making a decision."

"There's absolutely no need for that," she replied equally firmly.

The two parents were secretly relieved, although they did not show it. In this household there was no place for compulsion. The children were allowed an unusual amount of freedom and frankness. Even so, Munira's reasons for turning this man down were not based solely on the difference in age. The truth of the matter was that she had fallen in love, but no one had noticed yet; not even her mother who could sometimes see things with her heart as well as with her eyes.

This love of Munira's presented a real problem. She had fallen in love with a young man from Helwan, but had discovered that she was seven years older than he. He was still in secondary school and had failed several grades. But appearances were deceptive. The first time she had set eyes on him had been in the Japanese Garden. His eyes widened as he stared with a dumbfounded smile at this extraordinarily beautiful girl. He sat opposite her on the train, by deliberate choice, one must assume. In any case, he spent the entire journey back to Cairo sneaking glances at her. He looked a lot older than he actually was, and his masculine features had shown themselves long before their usual time. She assumed that he must be either a government employee or at least a student in his final year. In addition to all that, his features and voice all suggested a vigorous manhood. He started following her relentlessly; his kindness and determination managed to win her over. What he found was a heart fluttering its wings and longing for a first drop of water so that it could open its petals and reveal its flamboyant colors.

That is how he managed to win her heart. She gave herself up to love's melodious call while dreaming of happiness to come. It was when they were both standing in front of the sleeping statue of the Buddha in the peace and quiet of the Japanese Garden that she found herself engaged in a fierce struggle between the clashing demands of modesty and adventure. Eventually, however, she allowed herself to respond to one of his greetings.

"At long last!" he sighed. "God forgive you . . . ."

She felt flustered. "What do you want?" she stammered.

"No more than what my behavior must have made you realize," he replied calmly.

She had to bite on her lip to suppress a traitorous smile.

"Nothing's more important than love," he went on gently.

How right he is, she told herself. After that they used to meet often at the Genevoise, quite close to the university, so that they could get to know each other better. Their two families were alike. His father was a primary school inspector, and he had a married sister and a brother who was an army officer. His name was Suliman Bahgat. When he told her how old he was and that he was still in secondary school, it was the kind of blow she had not expected. After all, she was about to enter the English Department at the university; she might well have a job while he was still enrolled at the university. What a huge joke that would be, a real farce. Her mind was in turmoil, but her heart continued to show the resolve of lovers, tossing all impediments aside. Suliman noticed how disconsolate she looked and realized why.

"Love is never bothered by trivial problems," he said.

"Are they really that trivial?" she asked in despair.

"Certainly," he replied. "We must stay true to our love until we're married."

"You're serious," she replied, trying to suppress her happiness. "I have complete confidence in you. But I'm asking you

10

to wait a while so we can both think about it and make sure it's best for both of us."

"I'm quite sure that it is for me," he said, and then let out a laugh. "I'm not going to let you back out!"

The only person in her family in whom she could confide was her mother. After the evening prayer she entered her mother's green room and shut the door behind her.

"I have something to tell you, Mama," she said as she sat down.

When her mother realized that this was something really important, her heart initially lit up in delight. However, once the issue was explained, the light quickly went out. Staring straight at her daughter, she could immediately sense the secret purpose lurking behind her display of diffidence. In a panic she told herself that Kawthar's luck was definitely not going to be that good, but Munira was the family jewel. There was no way that her luck could turn out to be bad.

"It won't work," she said firmly. "There's nothing good about it."

Munira stared at her in utter misery.

"It's much better for the man to be older," she went on, "rather than the woman. Take care, Munira. This is simply a childish whim with nothing going for it. You're a sensible, well-educated girl."

Munira said nothing, and her mother realized the significance of her silence.

"People fall in love so they'll be happy, not to turn their lives into a laughingstock. No one will stop you from doing what you want. You're completely free to make your own choice, but I'm warning you. Women get older faster than men."

"Thank you, Mama," Munira muttered cryptically.

"There's no need to rush," her mother said hopefully. "Take your time and think about it. Leave things as they are until it's time to get married. Then you can see what the situation is like."

Munira felt totally disconsolate. "That's the best plan, Mama," she said.

"Fine. But let's keep the whole thing secret for the sake of family honor . . . ."

Even so the mother was not one to keep such an important matter a secret from Hamid Burhan. She told him about it before he went out for his evening gathering. His reaction to the news was only surpassed by her own worries that he would be even more emotional about it than she was or that he did not possess the same level of self-control.

"Oh Munira, my dear daughter!" he commented, addressing his wife in a plaintive tone, "what kind of fate is this supposed to be? Here she is, the crown jewel of our family. Why on earth is she getting herself involved in an escapade like this?" He paused for a moment's thought, and then went on, "At this point, we can see it as simply a foolish impulse, but later on it might cause problems when someone else comes to ask for her hand . . . ."

Saniya had no dreams pertinent to the subject, and Umm Sayyid's coffee-ground readings dealt with things far from this particular topic. For his part, Suliman Bahgat backed off his insistence that the engagement be announced immediately, making do with a relationship that seemed more like one between friends with its shared affection and cautious behavior, carefully nurtured with a good deal of patience. But in spite of everything, such a momentous secret could not stay that way for long. As long as there was a pungent odor in the air and receptive channels for spreading it, it could not remain so. Eventually it reached Suliman Bahgat's household.

"You've made a fine choice," Suliman's army-officer brother told him.

Many of Munira's friends at college knew Suliman. Eventually word reached all the way to Ibn Hawqal Street where it was the topic of conversation at the evening gathering.

That was the way that everyone near and far got to hear that Hamid Burhan's beautiful daughter was 'reserved.' As a result no one came to ask for her hand in marriage, and she became just like her sister, Kawthar, waiting for ages and growing ever older. It was wartime, days of sheer misery; death was the primary topic on the front pages of newspapers. On the broader scale, news came of the destruction of major cities and the imminent approach of danger to Egypt itself. Both Cairo and Alexandria were holding their breath.

"Compared with everywhere else," Hamid Burhan commented, "Egypt's situation is trivial."

Living standards collapsed and old pricing patterns disappeared forever. Family wealth went down the drain, leaving only government employees to survive at the bottom.

"What's the point of keeping track of a family budget," was Saniya's question, "when the whole thing's mere illusion?"

If the Wafd had not been brought back to power in the wake of a particularly severe crisis and if it had not decided to raise salaries to cope with inflation, government employees would have been totally ruined. Even so, the February 1942 incident did not in any way ruffle Hamid Burhan's basic loyalty to the Wafd; quite the contrary, the news made the entire evening gathering dance for joy, with a generous additional dose of malice toward the king.

"It's disgusting," was Munira's comment, "utterly unbelievable!"

"Everything I hear is disgraceful!" said Muhammad to his father.

"If there's a single phrase that deserves to be forever blown to smithereens," Hamid Burhan stated confidently, "then it's Mustafa al-Nahhas's nationalism."

Munira nodded. "You're right about that!" she responded with a smile.

Events took their course, and indications of victory swung in the other direction. As usual, the Wafd government was dismissed. Two years later Hamid Burhan reached retirement age and had to leave his job. That caused him a good deal of distress, so much so, in fact, that he felt as if he had died before his actual death. When he went home to Helwan and took off his official uniform for the first time as a retiree, he was really depressed. He felt somehow ashamed, as though he had committed a crime of some sort.

"I'm still fit and healthy," he told himself.

As he sat on the train to Helwan, he planned out a strategy that would confront the government's decision to pension him off. Every morning he would wake up at his usual time and take a walk in the area between the desert and the Japanese Garden, steeping himself in the dry, crisp air of Helwan. He would make sure to drink lots of mineral water and, to the extent that his now limited financial resources would permit, look after the garden. Saniya, in turn, welcomed him home and wished him a long life, all the while banishing a whole series of misgivings that buzzed around her insides like flies. She felt really sorry for him, noticing the depression that easily overwhelmed his phony attempts at laughter. In so doing she was giving him his fair share of attention, and yet she too was suffering the impact of the times. She had an innate fear of the unknown, coupled with her ongoing worries as mistress of the house, someone who had to perform the next-to-impossible in order to conserve as much as she could in the face of a lifestyle that was gradually but steadily becoming harder and harder to maintain. She kept giving all due thanks to God for the imminent graduation of Muhammad and Munira.

"They all started this war and went off," she said in a moment of contemplation. "Now we're the ones who have to pay the price . . . ."

Buying food and clothes used up the entire family budget. Didn't this huge house need any repairs or repainting, she wondered. And what about the garden, with its wilting trees and fading flowers? Not only that, but sandy soil covered a large part of the roof; didn't that need turning over? How did she feel about all of this? What was she supposed to do when she had to bear all the household responsibilities with no help, apart from a broken-hearted daughter and a maid of her own age who was only good at reading fortunes from coffee dregs— which in any case she didn't believe most of the time!

And yet problems can sometimes be superseded by others. This is exactly what happened to this household. Something happened that put warm smiles back on their faces. At long last a man came to ask for Kawthar's hand! Khalil al-Dars, a member of her father's evening group, was the one who arranged it all. The groom was none other than Nuaman al-Rashidi whose house manager Khalil was.

"He's a man like no other," was Khalil al-Dars's word to Hamid Burhan.

"Mind you," he went on quickly before Hamid's hopes rose too high, "he's not really educated, but then why does he need it? He's sixty years old, but he's as healthy as someone half that age. He has three sons, but they all have jobs and are married. He owns land and apartment blocks and has lots of money. He lives in a pretty villa on Zagazig Street in Heliopolis. His wife died a year ago, and he started feeling really lonely. The whole thing was getting him down, until I happened to suggest that he remarry. He welcomed the idea, far more, in fact, than I would have expected. So I asked my wife to invite Madame Saniya and Kawthar for a visit, and invited him as well. I arranged for him to get a look at her as she arrived and left. He was delighted and urged me to proceed. So here I am, carrying out my promised function . . . ."

So that was how all the problems of daily living vanished, and the new project came to dominate their hearts and hopes. Turning off the radio in the living room, Hamid Burhan broached the subject.

"So that's your husband-to-be. What do you say?"

Kawthar was on the point of leaving, but Hamid Burhan grabbed her by the arm and pulled her gently to his side.

"This is your place," he said.

"Fortunately," said Muhammad with a laugh, "the government doesn't interfere in such matters."

Saniya had some thoughts of her own. Why is it, she wondered, that my two daughters' luck always seems so complicated and never goes right?

"Let's leave the decision to the person who's primarily concerned!" she said.

"Of course, of course!' Hamid Burhan agreed. "But there's no harm in expressing an opinion as a way of helping her along. The man's certainly rich, and wealth is one of this life's greatest blessings!"

Muhammad was about to chime in with the rest of the Qur'anic verse but decided not to do so. For him, the very idea of his sister having to stay in the big family house with no husband, education, or work had already made him extremely worried.

"It's definitely an opportunity that should be seriously considered."

Now it was Munira's turn to speak. "I totally support Kawthar without conditions."

"But you haven't said anything yet!" said her father.

"I've said everything there is to say," replied Munira.

Hamid Burhan looked over at his wife who was sitting on the couch with her legs folded. Her gaze wandered, and she stared at the family photograph. Meanwhile, Kawthar was thinking to herself that they all seemed inclined to accept the offer. Actually, she herself had been similarly inclined from the outset. He was the first man who had offered her his hand. Here she was almost twenty-six years old, and things looked really desperate. She had hated all the sympathy and had felt too ashamed to receive female visitors.

"What about you, Kawthar?" her father asked gently.

She lowered her head. "I agree," she muttered.

The family gathering thus came to a serene conclusion. Even so, they all felt dogged by an uneasy sense of guilt, although they made every effort to resist it by resorting to all kinds of nice gestures.

"This decision's a blessing for everyone," was Hamid Burhan's remark to his wife, Saniya, once everyone else had left.

When she looked at him, she was shocked to see tears in his eyes, although she was not all that surprised. She was well aware of the way he cried whenever something really sensitive pulled at his heartstrings. For her part, she was crying inside.

"Why are you crying?" she asked him sadly.

"Because I feel so weak and unlucky," he replied with a deep sigh.

He was referring, of course, to his own financial straits and his daughter's ill fortune, being far more alert to realities than the people around him. He had watched with a heavy heart as Kawthar withdrew into herself, how sad she always looked, how she had suffered through adolescence, how desperately she involved herself in acts of worship, and how totally devoted she was to the ongoing process of serving her siblings in whatever way she could. All of which forced him to confront his own weakness. What had he ever done for her? What incentives did he have to help her? How he had suffered when she was going to school, insisting that she perform above her capacities, even though he himself had found learning as tough as she did and yet had not managed to identify any better way to bolster his own and his offspring's hopes for the future.

17

"So what do we do now?" he asked his wife and chief counselor.

Even from such a terse question she could guess what he was really getting at. "I have some pretty nice jewelry," she replied.

"And I can try to get a loan," he said meekly.

"You'll never find anyone to lend you money," she reacted angrily. "There's no need for that."

In any case Nuaman al-Rashidi managed to make such difficulties that much easier to deal with. He went to a great deal of trouble, for example, giving all the furniture in his villa to his children and then refurnishing it in the very latest style. Not only that, but he also agreed to accept a bridal dowry and a repayment plan that were both purely token gestures. The family was, needless to say, profoundly relieved by such generosity, but the negative side of the whole thing manifested itself in hurtful displays of sheer arrogance. For that very reason Kawthar's mother spent inordinate amounts of money on clothing of various styles and colors for her daughter and gave her a number of expensive gifts—gold bracelets, diamond earrings, and an antique watch. Nuaman al-Rashidi, aging aristocrat that he was, seemed anxious to have things settled, so he fixed a date for the marriage in the huge house. While many of his friends attended, not a single one of his own children was there, a gesture that proclaimed loud and clear that they would henceforth be severing all relations with their father. Once the ceremony was over, he took his bride with him in his white Mercedes, his smiles of farewell glazed with tears that signaled his mixed emotions.

"Thank God," said Hamid Burhan after the family's first visit to the villa on Zagazig Street. "Now Kawthar is happily settled!"

And she really was happy. She came to love her husband, and he reciprocated although in a somewhat restrained fashion.

But then, for Kawthar, any kind of love was love. Before too long she was able to give the family some good news, that there would be a new arrival. Needless to say, that brought a feeling of genuine joy to Saniya's heart, one that seemed perfumed with the lovely scent of roses. Kawthar adopted a new hairstyle that made her look much more feminine; with make-up on she even looked attractive. Expensive clothes gave her a new aura of staid elegance, although it should be pointed out that she still kept up her regular devotions. She did not tell her mother about a few minor concerns that had insinuated themselves into her consciousness, the origins of which were Nuaman al-Rashidi's desperate attempts to get her to drink a bit of whisky. His rationale for doing so consisted of a set of private legal opinions (which were, of course, completely without foundation) that drinking of this kind was permissible. However, he eventually gave up and simply acknowledged the ways things were.

No sooner had Hamid Burhan stopped worrying about Kawthar than his attention turned to the new apartment block that was being put up directly opposite his own home. The old house had been knocked down years earlier, and the foundations for the new building had been laid, but for some unknown reason all work on the site had stopped for some time. Now it had resumed. The wide base had been finished, and the large new structure had been built up on it. It all made Hamid very sad. He was sorry that the garden of the original house no longer existed and a huge new structure had risen in its place, blocking the view he had enjoyed for so long and impeding the free flow of air. New people started living in the apartment block, and their number soon exceeded that of all the other people living on Ibn Hawqal Street. Nobody knew anyone else, nor were they anxious to change the situation.

"This is what happens to old houses like ours," Gaafar Ibrahim commented.

"But what's to become of Helwan," Hamid Burhan asked, "if it loses its normal peace and quiet?"

Just then he had a thought: maybe the Buddha statue in the Japanese Garden would rouse itself and protest against the increased noise. It would then retreat to the desert in quest of some peace.

The new building was not the only worry either. The world of politics launched its own flood in his direction, in the form of student and worker demonstrations demanding a genuine level of independence that would match the sacrifices and services that Egypt had made during the course of the Second World War. As usual, politics dominated the evening group's conversation. As was to be expected, Hamid Burhan, the staunch Wafdist, plunged into a discussion of the issues involved.

"If Mustafa al-Nahhas stays in power," he said, "the English are bound to demand his support once the Germans are finally defeated."

Even so, political issues such as these did not stop him from noticing the new occupant of an apartment on the fourth floor of the new building. It was early fall. He happened to be strolling around his overgrown garden, doing his best to rid himself of the emptiness he kept feeling now that he had retired, when he turned around and noticed her walking along the street. She may have been about the same age as Saniya—about fifty—but she looked svelte and well turned-out, with gold-colored hair and foreign features. This brief glimpse of her aroused a frisson of excitement in him, something he had never felt before. After all, ever since he had married Saniya al-Mahdi, he had never even thought of looking at another woman. Throughout his married life he had been an ideal husband, unstinting and unchanging, never indulging in youthful dreams. In fact, so ingrained was this instinct that he had a wide reputation for it. None of his acquaintances could ever remember hearing him talk about other women.

His friend, Radi Abu al-Azm, the science teacher, put it this way: "Hamid is a specialist on his own wife."

It emerged that this woman had managed to arouse a good deal of interest among the neighbors, provoked, no doubt, by her European looks, her contemporary appearance, and her fashion sense. The melodious fountain of her very presence emitted a veritable spray of information: people said that her mother had been European—no one was quite sure which nationality. She was the widow of someone called Hasan Kamal, who had been a teacher at the Faculty of Law and earlier in his career a participant in a student mission abroad. She was said to have one daughter who was a translator at the Foreign Ministry. That particular piece of information was later revised, to the effect that she was actually her father's daughter by a previous wife who had died; this second wife had adopted her since she herself was barren—a decision that was considered a generous act on her part. Later they learned that her name—once she had converted to Islam—was Mervat, and the daughter's name was Ulfat.

The woman compensated for her loneliness by walking around Helwan and visiting the Japanese Garden. As she strolled around the garden, looking elegant, poised, and alluring, she managed to provoke—without even bothering about it—all kinds of thoughts. She would simply smile provocatively. By contrast, Ulfat concentrated on her job and was much more reserved and serious. Where Hamid Burhan was concerned, Mervat was not merely an exciting woman, but a raiding party launching an assault on his impregnable domestic fortress, a fire that had hit the dry straw of his imagination, a full-scale flood that was lapping at his own High Dam.

"Heaven help me!" he muttered to himself in amazement as he assessed his situation.

At that point he remembered the demonstrations and bloodshed that had taken place on the Cairo University campus and on the Abbas Bridge. "All of which confirms," he said, "that the earth really does revolve on a bull's horn!"

Things began to turn ugly when the woman started paying him some attention and made it quite clear that she was encouraging him. One day their eyes locked together, and she gave him a smile. With that, his willpower collapsed and all his innate instincts deserted him. His portly body was stirred by a burning insanity. Totally forgetting his own reality, Saniya, Kawthar, Muhammad, and Munira, he followed her into the Japanese Garden. He knew nothing about love or what the appropriate thing to say was on an occasion like this, so he simply gave way to a childlike innocence. They both agreed to meet in Cairo; as a precaution they chose to meet on the day he went to the city to collect his pension. With the beginning of this relationship, he found himself in a quandary: from the outset he was aware that his "expenses" would not allow him to maintain an illegitimate relationship, quite apart from the fact that they had not found a suitable love nest.

"I'm a respectable woman!" she told him.

They were sitting in Parliamo at the Pyramids.

"As you can see," he said with a telling frankness, "I'm not a wealthy man."

Her response was unusually bold. "I've a reasonable supply of private funds."

"Provided that my son and daughter both find jobs fairly soon," he said with a disarming naiveté, "I may be able to hold on to half my pension."

The conversation then turned to what should happen next. Hamid Burhan found himself hurled into a new life, the very notion of which had never once occurred to him.

"Now," he told himself on the way back to Helwan, "I can understand the real meaning of the phrase that says a man should be in control of his own affairs."

The bomb went off inside Saniya's heart, as her beloved husband of many years stood there weeping in front of her on the old, threadbare rug—back bent and eyes glazed.

"It's God will," he said, "and God alone has the power and might!"

She was aroused from her reverie by a sudden electric jolt that went straight through her. What was this crazy man saying?

"I've married again. It's all been an ordeal. But you will, of course, still be my wife and mother of my children!"

So what on earth could have happened?

"You must be crazy!" she said.

As usual when his emotions got the better of him, he had burst into tears. For her part, she maintained her normal air of calm, although it was certainly colored by a good deal of confusion. She had always hated and despised him when he cried, but now they were both on the edge of a cliff. She had a sudden urge to slap him, but she resisted the temptation and kept a tight control on her churning emotions. Her heart was the only thing that would be allowed to break, but it would all happen with no fuss. She decided to swallow the bitterest of pills as though the taste was sweetness itself.

"Nothing will ever separate us," he said, although his voice was that of someone else.

That was too much for her. "Never let me see your face again!" she yelled.

Muhammad and Munira were given the news.

"What a total disaster!" was Muhammad's reaction.

Munira said nothing, but burst into tears. Both of them stood firmly behind their mother and unconditionally condemned their father for his act of folly.

"I don't understand a thing," Munira told Muhammad as they stood alone together on the veranda.

"It's a total disaster," Muhammad commented angrily, "first for our father and then for our mother. Eventually it'll affect the entire family."

This second marriage led husband and wife to indulge in two different types of madness. In Saniya's case it took the form of silence and pride. She insisted on carrying on her daily life as if she simply did not care. However the truth of the matter was that her heart and mind were both in permanent turmoil. Behind normal daily events—whether heard or read about—she would detect the shadow of some vague cosmic tragedy. Humanity's basic stupidity was a chronic disease that could only be cured through a whole series of contradictions involving things like violence, common sense, and mercy. With the departure from the family home of the 'would-be-spry' old man, she found herself with spare time, something she had never had before. She turned her attention to the house and, more than ever before, came to the conclusion that it was not the way it should be; it had not been well looked after and was decaying before her eyes. She started going through all the rooms and the garden, looking and taking notes: faded paintwork, flaking plaster, floorboards cracking and warping. The garden had withered away, weeds had taken over, and desiccated leaves were piled up at various points.

"As the old saying goes," she told herself, "the eye may be able to see things, but unfortunately the hand is not up to the task!"

On one occasion Muhammad watched her as she wandered around. "I'm worried about her," he whispered in Munira's ear.

"So am I," Munira replied. "If only she could find something to distract her, even if it meant crying . . . ."

As for Hamid Burhan's madness, all he could do was to close his eyes and block his ears to the past and throw himself

24

into his newfound sea of honey. He turned himself into a gray-haired pseudo adolescent, with a body that managed to find some fresh vigor from who knows where. In Mervat he discovered a woman of sterling qualities who was expert in varieties of love-making that he had never encountered before. Both of them indulged in their passion for each other. Nevertheless the new relationship would not have survived but for the financial support that she was able to provide for their life together.

With the passage of time, the evening gathering moved to the new apartment. To the men's usual topics of conversation fresh items were added, including descriptions of the ways in which the younger generation was pursuing new paths. Rashad, Kawthar's son, was born; Muhammad graduated from the university, and Munira soon followed him. All these should have brought with them a good deal of joy, and yet such happiness proved to be very short-lived, the way clouds break up to reveal sunrise for just a few minutes on a particularly stormy day.

The general situation grew even more gloomy when the Palestine conflict broke out in 1948. The atmosphere was extremely tense, and the noise of battle easily drowned out the sexual conflicts that Hamid Burhan was going through. Saniya's condition went from bad to worse, as though she had only managed to rid herself of a painful headache to find herself afflicted with rheumatism. Munira kept up with the news from her new position as an English teacher at the Abbasiya School for Girls, while Muhammad got a job in the office of Counselor Abdel Qadir al-Qadri, the well-known Wafdist lawyer. He had been in contact with this lawyer during his earlier days as a loyal Wafdist, and he had not allowed the relationship to fade even when he had decided to add an ever-growing adherence to the Muslim Brotherhood to his former Wafdist tendencies. Muhammad went to great lengths to earn the trust of his employer and managed to do so. However, by the time the Palestine war had come to an end, the Arabs had lost, and Nuqrashi, the prime minister, had been assassinated. Now there was a declaration of all-out internal war on the Muslim Brotherhood, with no holds barred. Muhammad was one of the young men in Helwan who were arrested. The old house in Helwan now played host to Nuaman al-Rashidi and Kawthar and indeed to Hamid Burhan himself. Saniya studiously ignored him, and he had no desire to upset her. He therefore directed his remarks at Nuaman or Munira.

Hamid was no less worried than Saniya, but Nuaman tried his best to calm his fears.

"He hasn't committed any crime," he said, "that's for sure. So there's no need to worry too much . . . ."

"What I'm afraid of," said Munira, "is that they're so set on taking revenge that they're not going to discriminate between the innocent and the guilty."

"I've never been happy about his joining the Muslim Brother-hood," said Hamid Burhan. "After all, we're all Muslims, God be praised!"

Nuaman al-Rashidi was well aware that he was expected to do something more than just talk. After all, he was closely con-nected to officials in every political party.

"I'm going to do everything I can," he said, "even though in circumstances like these it's very risky to try to defend some-one who's a member of the Muslim Brotherhood."

He was eager to maintain his contacts with all the political parties, and it made him angry to think that his brother-in-law belonged to the Muslim Brotherhood. How was he supposed to conduct himself, he wondered, now that this shocking secret was known?

All of them felt particularly sorry for Saniya, realizing full well that she was the fulcrum for the family's sorrows.

"My trust in God remains unshaken!" she said sadly.

Nevertheless she became more and more morose and started sleeping badly. She might fall asleep, but her heart remained fully awake; and her dreams were wracked with pain. She received a letter from her brother informing her that his eldest son had actually been killed during the Palestine conflict when he had assumed that he was simply lost. She rushed to Beni Souef to console her brother on his great loss.

After some time had passed, Muhammad was released. One day he came home, threw himself into his mother's arms, and made a big show of being happy—in spite of how thin and pale he looked—in the process keeping the awful facts about his imprisonment hidden from her. He went back to his job with Abdel Qadir al-Qadri, determined to put his best efforts into it.

"So," his boss asked him, "have you had enough of the Brotherhood by now?"

"Quite the opposite," he replied with a laugh.

"You need to understand what the Wafd's really about before it's too late. It's not a political party, but rather the foundation for a cohesive framework. In a word, it's Egypt itself."

"Are we supposed to spend the rest of our lives fussing about independence and the constitution?"

"Fine, be as modern as you like, but do it within the framework of the Wafdist base, or else you'll find yourself back in the pre-imprisonment era!"

When Muhammad and Munira were alone together, she expressed her real feelings. "You look so thin!" she said sadly.

"I'll never forget the pain I went through," he responded with a frown. "The lashes fell all over my body like rain."

Saniya had guessed as much for herself, inspired in part by her nightmares. Even so, she decided to tough things out in this new existence she was living. She dispelled all thoughts of

Hamid Burhan from her soul, like someone spitting out a sweet that turns out to be sour. And yet, with all that, he still stayed with her like an open wound, as she rued the loss of earlier days of love and loyalty. She told herself to forget the past and find her own consolation. If she could only find a way at some point of restoring the old house to its former youthful glory, she might even be happy. She had half of the 'traitor's' pension to live on, along with the salaries of both Muhammad and Munira, but inflation was continuing its inexorable march. In any case, both Muhammad and Munira had to have their own private hopes for the future. All that was left was her dreams, rebuilding and repainting the house, selling the old furniture and buying some new. Beyond all such dreams, she still needed to cut the grass, nurture the roots, fertilize the soil, and plant the rose seedlings. She kept invoking the spirits of saints and ancestors; by doing so, she was confronting her memories which insisted on subverting her own intentions. That made her hurl thunderbolts at wonderful memories that almost inevitably seemed to be gleaming on the horizon.

"If it looks good," she told herself, "then be very careful!"

Munira had her own series of issues to address. She learned that Bahgat Suliman had done reasonably well in his agricultural studies and was now employed in the Ministry of Agriculture. They were still sticking to their agreement.

"It's all in God's hands," she told herself.

Muhammad was still convalescing after his imprisonment and trying to decide on his career. The Brotherhood no longer existed as such, but religion remained his principal reading focus. From it he gleaned an entirely new attitude to religion, one that differed from that of his family—which had previously been characterized by its tolerance and simplicity. After his release from prison he had asked his mother for permission to spend some time with his father. He had spent a good hour or so with him, in the company of Mervat Hanem and Miss Ulfat. For the first time he had observed Ulfat from close up, and she had managed to stir his innocent heart. When he left, she had been wrapped in a virtual cloak of affection. He saw her on the train; indeed he often sat with her and they exchanged conversation. As a result, she was always present in his memory and imagination; whether it was the house, office, or law court, she was there with him, and his reaction was always a positive one. His heart would give a flutter of sheer joy, but then he would inevitably have to face the major question.

"But what about Mama?"

However, just then the public arena surprised him by offering a totally unexpected occasion for joy: the Ministry resigned, and free elections loomed on the horizon as a distinct possibility.

"Good God," was Muhammad's reaction, "let's not get too slap-happy!"

But Hamid Burhan was fairly dancing for joy. He and Muhammad found themselves united in a single circle of election talk.

"Thank God," he whispered in his son's ear, "you're still a Wafdist at heart!"

"In these elections," Muhammad replied, "the Brotherhood are with the Wafdists!"

So the Wafd was returned to power, and once again Hamid Burhan mounted his throne. "So eternity in this world of ours is a real possibility," he declaimed.

Halcyon days returned, and people believed that the era of misery had come to an end. Munira started thinking about her future with her abiding love affair in mind, while love bound Muhammad and Ulfat together as well. The two of them decided to get married but at the same time to postpone the announcement until the time was right. However, just at that point negotiations aimed at adjusting the terms of the 1936 Treaty of Montreux broke down, and a period of uncertainty ensued until the voice of Mustafa al-Nahhas rang out with the call to annul the entire treaty. At the evening gathering in Mervat Hanem's apartment enthusiasm reached a high pitch, leading Hamid Burhan to recall that he had felt just as enthusiastic on the day the treaty was signed as he did now when it was liable to be annulled.

"If Egypt was supposed to be the bride in 1936, what's to happen in 1951?!"

"Things happen fast these days," commented Khalil al-Dars, "and change comes just as quickly!"

"The only people able to annul the treaty," Hamid Burhan went on, "are the people who signed it in the first place. And that's the Wafd . . . onward and forever!"

What followed was a period of conflict and sacrifice as fires gripped various parts of Cairo.

"A curse on such traitors!" Hamid Burhan commented to Mervat.

She did not share his opinions. "Helwan's far removed from such problems," she said.

Saniya stood on the roof of the house looking in the direction of Cairo through a telescope that Muhammad had won as a boy in a lottery at the Olympia Cinema.

"Dear Lord," she told herself anxiously, "please remove Your anger and hatred from us . . . !"

When the very face of Cairo itself flared in furious anger and threatened the direst of consequences, Muhammad went to the Ministry of Foreign Affairs and accompanied Ulfat to the Bab al-Luq Station.

"I'm afraid all transport's going to come to a halt," he said.

They both returned home before they realized the true extent of the danger that was relentlessly chewing up an entire page in a history book already stained with blood. When it came, the reaction was savage and struck like a thunderbolt.

"The criminals are laughing themselves hoarse!" was Hamid Burhan's comment.

But the laughter came to an abrupt halt when a new voice made itself heard early on the morning of July 23rd, 1952. The family was sitting around the breakfast table as they listened and exchanged glances.

"Let's hope for the best," Muhammad said. "It's got to be better than the way things were!"

"What about the English?" asked Munira.

At this point Saniya chimed in. "Any kind of hope, however vague, has to be better than utter despair!"

Hamid Burhan proceeded to follow the rapid course of events with considerable dismay. As a Wafdist, he had always participated in events, for good or ill, when the field involved the Wafd and its opponents. But this time effective power lay with an unfamiliar, recently formed group, one with unclear intentions at that. He watched as the ancient foe—the king— went into exile forever, but he had no idea whether to regard that as a victory or defeat. He grew listless and felt distinctly uneasy, and for reasons he could not identify.

"Those are the wages of frivolity!" he muttered mechanically as he noticed the way Mervat was crying at the king's departure.

"Don't you realize," she asked him, "that power has devolved to someone who has placed himself above the law?!"

"But they're promising to respect the constitution," he replied, not believing a single word he was saying.

Just like Mervat, Kawthar wept when she heard that the king had been exiled. For the first time in his life, Nuaman al-Rashidi quoted the Qur'an: "When the earthquake happens . . . and mankind asks, 'What is the matter?'"

For her part, Munira was completely and instinctively enthusiastic about the new political developments, the more so because she was influenced by her boyfriend, Suliman Bahgat, whose brother emerged as being one of the Free Officers. Muhammad was of a like mind, once he had made sure that the new movement was sympathetic to the Muslim Brotherhood; in fact he was invited to inject some new energy into the Helwan group. Hamid Burhan now summoned his son to an urgent meeting, knowing full well how things were going between Muhammad and Ulfat.

"Leave the Brotherhood," his father said. "You've already had enough trouble because of your innocent involvement with them."

"How on earth can I abandon them now," Muhammad asked in amazement, "just when they've won a tremendous victory?"

"It's a movement with no popular roots," his father said, suppressing his anger. "Don't let yourself fall prey to popular anger now as happened last time with the government."

"But that past is dead now," replied Muhammad with a confident smile, "before it even had a chance to kill off the movement . . . ."

The family was of the opinion that it already had a member in the new governing movement, thus allowing it to move from obscurity into a position of authority or even participation in the government itself. Munira thought she had two members, her own brother and her boyfriend. Saniya now felt much happier, having convinced herself that her dream of rebuilding the house would now happen in short order and, as day followed day, her troubles would lessen. Her private sorrows would gradually diminish as part of the general sense of excitement. Even Muhammad changed his mode of talking, using the first person much more than the third: "We're going to do this and that," he kept saying. Ulfat was eager for him to shine like all the others, her hope being that, if he managed to do so, they would be able to counter all the difficulties that stood in the way of their getting married. Without even realizing it, she too started to take an interest in politics and religion, using Muhammad as her yardstick and guide.

"How different she is from that frivolous mother of hers!" Muhammad thought to himself.

"How do you think Mama would react," he asked Munira one day, "if I told her about my relationship with Ulfat?"

Munira's reply shocked him. "I've already told her, as an act of mercy!"

"But I've not noticed any change in her attitude toward me!"

"Don't you know your own mother?"

In fact, Saniya had seen Ulfat several times through the window of her green-painted bedroom. As usual she had guessed what was going on and had braced herself to accept the inevitable. She told herself that her own luck was certainly better than that of the Queen of Egypt; it would be stupid to stand in the way of events that had the stamp of fate embossed on them. But how could she restore the house to its former youthful glory? That was destined to remain a dream. Meanwhile all she could do was worship God.

One evening Hamid Burhan was exploring the byways of the political situation at their regular meeting.

"This new movement is an American conspiracy," he said, "aimed at finishing off the Wafd once and for all."

He wanted to go on and expound on his position, but all of a sudden his energy flagged and he stopped talking. His face turned pale. Even though it was cold, he started sweating. Then his entire corpulent frame collapsed onto the black couch.

"What's the matter?" Hasan Alama, the architect, asked anxiously.

He tried to smile but failed; his faculties had completely deserted him. The Buddha's face loomed before his eyes, and his eyelids closed. They carried him to his bed. Mervat called the local doctor who soon diagnosed the event as a heart attack and ordered complete rest. Family and companions alike were taken aback. There was a wide variety of explanations, including the nonstop excitement of politics and the effects of his second marriage. It was Gaafar Ibrahim who had the final word, saying, "It's God's will."

Once the news had spread beyond the walls of Mervat's apartment, Munira, Muhammad, Kawthar, and Nuaman al-Rashidi all came by as well. Even Saniya al-Mahdi made her way there. In spite of everything that had happened, she had still been unable to erase her husband from her heart altogether. For sure, her chest tightened as she crossed the threshold of her rival Mervat's stronghold, but for the very first time she made herself shake hands with Mervat and Ulfat.

"Take courage!" she whispered as she leaned over her husband.

He gave her a grateful smile. Meanwhile, the entire atmosphere was fraught with a barely concealed tension. The usual category of pleasantries found themselves competing with underlying feelings of outright antagonism. Mervat realized that, from now on, not a day would pass without her life being ruined by the sight of a collection of faces that she could not stand. Hamid Burhan's condition had gone on for a while and was clearly destined to continue for even longer. He would never recover his former energy. For a lively woman like Mervat his illness had turned into a huge burden. In spite of everything, however, Hamid Burhan's condition had done nothing to lessen his sensitivities, and he soon came to realize that from now on he would be a stranger in his own bed. He began to feel unhappy about his situation, all of which led him one day to broach the subject with his son, Muhammad.

34

"I want to sleep at your place," he whispered.

Muhammad replied loud enough for Mervat to hear as well. "If you sleep at our place," he said, "it will save us the trouble of this never-ending series of visits!"

Mervat realized full well the point of what he was saying. "I'm always ready to help," she said, doing her best to conceal her own delight, "however long it takes."

"There's no doubt about that," replied Muhammad, reflecting the fact that he himself was in the process of getting married to her daughter. "But there are a lot of us, whereas you're on your own."

"I'm happy with whatever keeps him at peace," she replied cleverly, effectively putting an end to her relationship with him.

Saniya had no objections. Her sorrow over Hamid Burhan's serious illness was tempered by her delight at his admission that he would prefer her as his caregiver and companion and that her house was where he really wanted to be. Thus did Hamid Burhan return to his old bed in the green bedroom, a serene expression clearly visible in his lovely eyes. By now his body had shrunk to almost nothing, and his face showed all the signs of old age, almost as though it had arrived in a flash. Looking all around him, he seemed all of a sudden utterly content.

"Children," he said falteringly, "we've been apart for too long!"

The words were not specifically directed at Saniya, since he assumed that the very fact that he had come home made that unnecessary. Truth to tell, no sooner had his passion run its full course than he discovered that the only thing left was her abiding love. It was like some buried treasure uncovered below the earth's surface. Now, provided that fate allowed, his soul had to raise itself up from that former blessed place where it had resided, a spot perfumed by the most fragrant of memories.

Kawthar stared at him for a while, but could stand it no longer. "You've changed a lot, Papa!" she said with tears in her eyes.

Everyone there frowned, but Hamid Burhan simply smiled.

"But what about you, my daughter?" he asked a bit sluggishly. "Aren't you a mother now?!"

Everyone was delighted that he seemed so at ease and to be enjoying being back in his old home with his friends. Then came a day when the summer heat was at its height.

"I haven't been to the baths for ages," he said.

"We should consult the doctor," Munira suggested gently.

"A man can be his own doctor," was his happy response.

So he went to the baths, leaning on Saniya and Muhammad. He felt the water coursing over his body and felt all the pleasure of someone who had always wanted to be clean and neat.

"Someone who isn't healthy," he said happily as he went to bed, "is worse than an insect."

But when nighttime came, he could not sleep. His health deteriorated at an alarming rate, and he looked pale and gaunt. He spent the entire night groaning, his body twisting and turning. The doctor was called and protested that the visit to the baths had been a bad idea. In spite of that, he wrote him a prescription. At about midnight, with his family watching, he passed away without any pain; it was as if he had suddenly fallen asleep, looking very sad because everyone was making such a fuss over him.

Saniya was more devastated by his death than anyone could have imagined. Since he himself did not own a grave, he was laid to rest in the al-Mahdi family tomb in the cemetery of Imam Shafie. Saniya was very dissatisfied with the state of the grave and felt that it needed just as much fixing-up as did the old house in Helwan, all of which merely added to the anxieties that had been troubling her in recent times. But it was Kawthar who of all the children was the most sad, not only because by temperament she was someone who responded to grief in an unusual way, but also because she loved her father to the point

36

of adoration; in fact, she had forgiven her father for marrying Mervat long before Muhammad and Munira had.

As summer was beginning, death made another appearance, this time snatching away Nuaman al-Rashidi, Kawthar's husband, with kidney failure. His death may actually have brought him a certain relief from all the anxiety he was feeling because of the revolution. In fact, the Agricultural Reform Laws barely touched him because the bulk of his wealth was based on buildings and liquid assets. Even so, he was convinced that his turn would come, sooner or later—no doubt about it. Kawthar wept tears of sincere sorrow for her husband, but she soon shook out of it when his children started harassing her. Her brother Muhammad was soon by her side with his lawyer's expertise.

From the very first day she was explicit. "Spare me all these nasty confrontations," she said. "There's nothing in the world to equal the distress I'm feeling."

"You're going to get every single millieme you're entitled to!" Muhammad replied assertively.

"My rights are guaranteed under law," she pleaded, "but it's the villa they're after. It's enormous, and I don't feel safe living there by myself. I want to go back to Helwan and live with Mama."

So Kawthar returned to the house in Helwan, carrying her son, Rashad, in her arms. Meanwhile Muhammad set about securing her rightful inheritance and that of her son, which consisted of land, buildings, and liquid assets. With that settled, the relationship with the Rashidi family was forever severed. The Burhan family was secretly delighted that Kawthar had become so wealthy. They nursed their individual hopes with the thought that she was known to them all as a sweet and modest person. As a result they regarded her as a gift sent down from heaven, bringing with her relief from all their various problems and crises. By now Munira was almost thirty and expecting to get married, while Muhammad felt that his engagement had gone on for too long. And Saniya was eager to rebuild both the house and the family grave. They all managed to restrain themselves until the mourning period was over, but, once the dark clouds had passed and the radio once again started broadcasting its songs, Saniya plucked up her courage.

"My darling," she asked Kawthar somewhat bashfully, "don't you think the house needs some work?"

Muhammad realized at once that there was something that threatened to interfere with his own plans. He stole a swift glance at Munira and noticed that they were both having the same thought.

"There's nothing the matter with the house," he said. "It can wait."

"But it's always been our home," Saniya protested.

Muhammad now summoned the kind of blunt talk he had learned in court. "What both of us need," he said, pointing to both Munira and himself, "is financial support, not the house."

"Even if it's only a loan," he continued so as to soften the implications of what he was saying.

Faced with the demands of both Munira and Muhammad, Saniya withdrew, postponing her dreams for the house to some unknown date in the future.

"Even if it's just a loan!" repeated Munira with a laugh.

However, in spite of Kawthar's innate sweetness, she was still essentially a housewife who was working to help her mother. From her, Kawthar had learned to stick to a budget, watch expenses, and avoid excessive purchases. She was sweet and prudent at the same time. From her very first day back at the house she had been helping with the household budget, which had made things a lot easier and brought some much-needed serenity to the general atmosphere. Even so, she was not insensitive to the problems that Munira and Muhammad were facing and was inclined to offer them the funds they needed. She promised to do that, but it so happened that only three months after her husband's death, a matchmaker brought a new and highly respectable prospective husband of her own age for her to meet. Muhammad's and Munira's hearts both sank.

"We need to make sure that he's sincere," said Muhammad in his counselor's tone of voice.

Luckily for both of them, however, Kawthar announced that she would not be remarrying. Instead she intended to devote her life to Rashad who constituted her entire universe. In so doing, she adopted a reserve that was somewhat akin to frigidity. In any case, she made it possible for Munira to marry Bahgat Suliman and for Muhammad to wed Ulfat. In Munira's case the wedding was the consequence of a real love story, and she located a nice apartment in Abbasiya close to the school where she taught. Muhammad began his married life in an apartment in a fairly new building in Bab al-Luq so that he could both be close to the office where he was working and keep up his political activities at its hub.

As a result of all this, the old house was a lot emptier; only Saniya, Kawthar, Rashad, and Umm Sayyid were still living there. Kawthar had inherited her mother's observant eye and secret aspirations. She had the house repainted and the garden cleaned up, and bought some pots of carnations. But, in spite of these improvements, only a tiny portion of Saniya's dreams for the house were actually fulfilled. Even so, she was happy enough and still nursed the hope that one day she would be the recipient of God's mercy. That was particularly so when Rashad grew up to be a handsome boy, and started inviting his friends to the house just as Hamid Burhan had done before him. Saniya was so happy with these sudden improvements that she plucked up her courage one day and dropped a subtle hint about the family grave.

"Mama," Kawthar responded, "such talk strikes me as a bad omen!"

Saniya was sorry she had raised the topic and said nothing. "So it's to be just the house," she told herself. Even so she felt extremely grateful to her daughter. Now that Munira and Muhammad were both married, she might have had to live on her own and sponge off her children; that would have made her entire life as bleak as the frustration of her dreams. So, praise be to God! What made her happy as well was that both Munira's and Muhammad's marriages were going well, something she picked up from her visits to Bab al-Luq and Abbasiya.

"Bahgat certainly showed how loyal he was by waiting so long," she said to Kawthar one day, "but I'm not so sure about Mervat's stepdaughter."

"Muhammad knows how to handle things," was Kawthar's muted response.

Once Munira had settled happily into her married life, she became even more successful as a teacher. After Counselor Abdel Qadir al-Qadri had emerged from several prison terms because of his Wafdist affiliations, he invited Muhammad to become a partner in his office.

"Being a Wafdist is now a crime," he told Muhammad one day. "Mark well and inwardly digest!"

Muhammad started to panic a bit while he waited to see how the revolution would reveal its true colors, proclaiming, he hoped, the validity of Islam as the state institution that would occupy its legitimate place in the future. This aspiration was not merely some personal whim on his part, but represented the consequence of a genuine religious experience, something he had been drawn to in an amateurish fashion and almost by

40

accident. He continued to dream of Islam as the ruling principle as though it were the goal of all his desires.

Muhammad fathered two children, Shafiq and Siham, while Munira gave birth to Amin and Ali. The horizon was now looking very rosy. But then the revolution found itself confronting a crisis involving a fierce struggle between the first president and the second. Everything was in a state of flux, with factions pulling in opposite directions: one almost purging the revolution itself, while another took it back to its very bases. Amid all the chaos a tidal wave appeared to sweep away the Muslim Brotherhood! So, instead of Muhammad finding himself head of an association or ministry, he was thrown into a terrible prison. There was no specific charge against him, and yet he still spent two years in jail and emerged from the experience with only one eye and a crippled leg. Everyone rushed to the apartment in Bab al-Luq, where Saniya and Mervat met for the fourth time.

"It seems to be my bad luck," Saniya thought to herself. "I only get to see her when there's been a disaster of some kind."

"Your reckoning is only with God Almighty, my son," she sobbed as she hugged him to her bosom.

At first Muhammad put on a brave face so as to avoid talking about death and suffering, but, since everyone was staring at him, he plucked up the necessary courage.

"I'm luckier than a lot of people," he said. "Other people were hanged or disappeared into the depths of prisons forevermore . . . ."

He did his best to smile. "I still have my faith," he said insistently. "It remains unshaken."

However his insistence was stronger than his voice. By now he was very familiar with the ways of life and people and equally well acquainted with barbarity and pain. From his family he drew a strength that enabled him to light a candle

41

and shed some light on a world writhing in darkness. He happened to look over at Ulfat. Clasping her hand, he hoisted it into the air, something he regularly did whenever he was in a public gathering.

"Let me present to you," he would say, "the very best wife in the entire world!"

Yes indeed, she had remained steadfast throughout the entire trial. She had kept up her duties as both translator and housewife. She had carefully nurtured Shafiq and Siham, in the process confronting ostracism, various investigations, and very limited means of income. She had proved beyond any doubt that she was much stronger than either Muhammad or Mervat had imagined. She had maintained a steadfast love for her absent husband and had become still more committed to his principles. When he returned to her as a fractured shadow of his former self, she lavished all her love and affection on him, shining in his grim universe like a diamond star. Throughout his two-year imprisonment Kawthar had made a point of visiting her regularly and had offered her any assistance she needed, but Ulfat had gratefully refused the offer, although she did accept presents for Shafiq and Siham.

"Ulfat is a rare gift indeed," Kawthar told her mother during those sad times.

"Yes, I thank God," Saniya commented for the first time, much to her daughter's surprise, "I thank God that she's not made of the same stuff as her stepmother!"

The reason for her negative attitude toward Mervat was not only the disaster in the past, but also the fact that, following Hamid Burhan's death, Mervat had gone back to her former frivolous ways, thus becoming the talk of Helwan. Even though she was fifty-five years old, she was dolling herself up to look much younger. She used to go out on her own, either to the Japanese Garden or else to the cinema. It was as if she would willingly offer herself to any passer-by. Rumors soon spread that she was having an affair with Hasan Alama, the architect, who had been one of Hamid Burhan's evening companions. Once the word got around and everyone knew about it, the relationship turned into an engagement. The architect divorced his wife, but the wedding was postponed out of respect for Ulfat's husband, Muhammad, who was in prison (even though in fact they acted as though they were married, albeit in an unofficial way).

Kawthar was as aware of the sordid details as anyone else, but she still defended her sister-in-law. "Thanks be to God," she said, "Ulfat's cut from a different cloth!"

Muhammad was kept in the dark about this development. After a short period of convalescence, he went back to his old office, with his one good eye and a second glass one and with a heart fully poised and ready to start working again. He used to make his way to the law courts, limping and holding his briefcase under one arm while leaning on a thick cane that he held in his other hand. He plunged into his work with all the energy of a tormented believer dreaming that Noah's flood would happen all over again.

Saniya, meanwhile, carried on living with her pitiless sorrows and relentless dreams, the impossibility of which she accepted with a serene patience, a posture that from time to time was marked by a glance at that commemorative photograph on the wall. Kawthar was eager to relieve her mother of some of these problems, so she hired a new woman, Umm Gaber, to serve as cook; by this point Umm Sayyid, like Saniya herself, was approaching sixty. She was also keen to make the most of the time she had to take care of young Rashad, who by now was enrolled in kindergarten, something that put him ahead of his various cousins, Shafiq and Siham, Muhammad's children, and Amin and Ali, Munira's.

Thus began the era of grandchildren, participants in passion and pain. As far as the nation was concerned, it found itself pulled this way and that by a number of hidden factors but also by a few more obvious feats of heroism. Munira got to know her husband better and better, a passionate man and strong personality, but at the same time somewhat naïve when it came to matters of culture and public life. For that reason she refused to be deceived by his sudden interest in politics once he discovered that his own brother was one of the Free Officers who had engineered the revolution. Whenever he spoke about the revolution and the men involved in it and criticized the corruption of the past, she allowed herself a quiet chuckle.

"We're regarded as a family that's part of the new ruling class," he told Munira proudly one day.

"Take it slowly, my prince!" she replied with a laugh.

In fact Munira had supported the revolution from the outset. She had not changed her mind even after her own brother had been so badly treated—something that shook her to the core. Even so, once she was over thirty, she began to feel uneasy. She started carving out her own path, leaving behind her husband who was turning into even more of a flashy show-off. She would regularly act on the basis of advice that her mother had given her in times past whenever relevant situations arose.

With a strong recommendation from his brother, Suliman Bahgat was given a senior position in the technical division of the Agriculture Ministry. However, instead of contributing a larger share to the household budget, he bought himself a car on an installment plan, even though Amin and Ali had just started kindergarten and prices were slowly but relentlessly rising.

Then came the evening when a news bomb exploded: the nationalization of the Suez Canal and the emergence of a new leader.

"I've been told by one of the old folks," Suliman Bahgat confided in his wife, "that Gamal Abdel Nasser's welcome when he returned to Cairo was even greater than that of Saad Zaghlul when he returned from exile . . . ."

Munira agreed with him without hesitation, even though in fact she knew next to nothing about Saad Zaghlul. Muhammad on the other hand still had the bitter taste of his dreadful prison experiences in his mouth, so he was unable to share the joy of the moment with the same level of enthusiasm.

"Treating people decently," said Ulfat, sharing her husband's opinion, "is much better than building yourself another pyramid."

"The Prophet of God—peace and blessings upon him," said Muhammad, "founded a humane society. He didn't need to build a pyramid!"

The people in the old house in Helwan listened to the important news. Neither Umm Sayyid nor Umm Gaber understood a thing. For a minute Kawthar stopped teaching Rashad, but then resumed her task with the same enthusiasm. Saniya's ongoing sorrows and dreams did not stop her reading newspapers and listening to the radio. Her heart did a flutter, and she felt convinced that, in spite of the terrible experience that Muhammad had gone through, a new leader was now taking his place on the honor-roll of rulers whom she had loved, as had her late husband. The whole country enjoyed the intoxicating sense of victory and prestige. From the radio station Voice of the Arabs, a new Arab leadership made itself known. There were various news reports, and rumors ran amok. Eventually, however, the truth took concrete form in the threefold attack; enemy planes crisscrossed the Cairo sky day and night, raining their bombs on airports and military targets. Even though tanks were positioned in the courtyards of apartment blocks, national triumphs kept filling the air like thunderstorms. People found their emotions torn between outright enthusiasm and a degree of circumspection.

Both Muhammad and Ulfat were following the news on foreign radio stations.

"The regime of these criminals is at an end," said Muhammad. "But what a price to pay!"

Saniya shared her thoughts with her daughter. "My ear is happy, but my heart is sad."

"The country's been destroyed, Mama," was Kawthar's response.

"But He is still up there!" muttered Saniya, looking up at the ceiling.

Munira noticed that Suliman Bahgat was in total panic, like a cornered mouse.

"O God," he said in a fervent prayer to his God, "don't allow our enemies to gloat!"

Both of them were listening gloomily to the Voice of America and gradually sinking into an abyss of depression. However, winds started to blow from both east and west, and for the first time ever they came together. America steadfastly refused to accept the idea of the threefold invasion, and threats from Russia followed soon afterward like rockets. As a result, the invaders were forced to annul their would-be triumph and retreat in an episode of unprecedented humiliation. What emerged was a truly stunning victory. It was just like the girl who is used by a conjurer with his box; he plunges the sword in from every side while everyone watches, but she emerges from the box looking completely happy, serene, and confident!

Pretty soon every single Egyptian knew for sure that this new leader of theirs had achieved a miraculous victory; in fact, he stood out as a real giant among pygmies. French and English reserves were sequestered, a move that with a single stroke taught the aggressors a real lesson and provided the Arab people with a powerful leadership. As a result every citizen of Egypt felt able to remove the humiliation of ages from his

46

shoulders while the enemy hid in their holes, with no strategy in mind other than forgetting the whole thing.

The family's grandchildren now entered primary school, duly singing the praises of the country's leaders and the great victory that had been won. They swam in the pure waters of a Nasserite lake, gazing up at his photograph on the wall with love and glowing pride. Here now was a leader with whom history could really begin, a history that could take over from a prehistoric period of ignorance whose dark shadows extended back into the far-distant past. True enough, these new schools were not without their problems: huge numbers of students, not enough qualified teachers, and a shortage of programs. But the students were not aware of such things; it was only the authorities who realized the difficulties involved. Kawthar solved the problem by using her money to hire Gaafar Ibrahim, a retired school inspector and former member of Hamid Burhan's evening company, to give Rashad private lessons in Arabic, geography, and history, and Professor Radi Abu al-Azm, a member of the same group, to teach him science and math. Muhammad and Ulfat took time out from their already heavy schedules to spend hours helping Shafiq and Siham with their homework, while Munira took on the task of teaching Amin and Ali on her own.

There was something else that managed to annoy Madame Mervat as well.

"How can you be happy," she asked Ulfat, "to see Shafiq and Siham sitting down in class alongside children of doormen and servants?"

"Language academies and private schools are incredibly expensive," was Ulfat's reply.

Muhammad had other reasons for feeling annoyed when he took a look at the history textbooks and the new national school curricula.

"They're stuffing the kids' minds full of lies," he commented, throwing his hands up in disgust.

Muhammad's anger intensified as he watched the way Shafiq and Siham were so enthusiastic about the new leader, singing his praises in front of him. However, there was nothing he could do about it because he was concerned not only about their safety, but also his own. He needed to be sure they did not repeat in school the things he might tell them at home, which might lead to some nasty consequences. With that idea in mind, he kept his annoyance to himself.

"So now here we are," he muttered, "living in an era of compulsory silence!"

Rashad grew up to be a handsome boy, tall, nimble, and elegant. He adored his mother and grandmother and was fond of swimming. When it came to his studies, he had only moderate success, and his cousins were soon at the same level. His grandmother favored him over her other grandchildren, Shafiq, Siham, Amin, and Ali, not least because he was closest to her heart and person, not to mention the fact that his beloved mother was her favorite child. It was on him that she was pinning all her hopes to have the house and gravesite renovated. True enough, in his grandmother's eyes Rashad was like his cousins, Shafiq, Siham, Amin, and Ali, in that they all seemed like creatures with no roots. What is more, he did not seem to be breathing the same air in her old house. As an illustration, there was the first time he heard the name Saad Zaghlul mentioned.

"Is Saad Zaghlul still alive, Mama?" he asked in all innocence.

Even though Saniya came up with a number of pretexts to excuse his ignorance, she was still shocked. She was also unhappy about the indifferent way he reacted to Umm Kulthum's and Abdel Wahhab's singing and preferred Abdel

Halim Hafiz and western songs. She wondered to herself how this young man could have developed such a negative attitude toward his own family's traditions and tastes.

"They're all annoying," she told herself resignedly, "but then, every generation has its own agenda!" It was her genuine love of Rashad that led her to add, "And then, even a certain amount of variety has its own attractions!"

Of all the grandchildren Shafiq was the one who most resembled Hamid Burhan. He had a decent voice and regularly mimicked popular singers. He was a hard worker too, which suggested he would do well at school, but he was also very emotional. Sometimes that managed to annoy his father, who had to intervene whenever he tried to dominate his sister, Siham. For her part, Siham was a carbon copy of her aunt, Munira: radiantly beautiful and extremely intelligent, all of which made Muhammad very happy. As for Munira's two sons, Amin was known to be hard-working while Ali was recalcitrant. Both of them were widely recognized for being extremely tall.

"Just like my father," was Suliman Bahgat's comment.

Muhammad and Munira—along with their families—got into the habit of having Friday lunch at the old house with Saniya, Kawthar, and Rashad. The children got to know each other well, and the differences between them and their elders soon became evident. These regular visits delighted Saniya and helped her compensate for the dreams and persistent hopes for the future that she kept buried inside her.

Since those aspirations of hers were clearly not going to be fulfilled, she transferred her attention for the moment to her own person. Apparently without any forethought or planning, it all fell into place bit by bit; it was as though she had made up her mind to protect herself against the ravages of time. There was the occasion when she did not like the way her teeth looked, so she went to the dentist to have them cleaned, filled, and coated. Then her eye gave a twitch while she was reading, so she went to see the ophthalmologist who gave her some glasses.

For her part, Kawthar became more and more ascetic. Devoting herself wholeheartedly to worship, she grew old before her time. Even though Saniya was devout and God-fearing, she still was upset when the first gray hair showed itself in the midst of her profusion of black. The very image of old age was anathema to her since she saw it as being completely out of place in view of her otherwise excellent health. She immediately revived a custom her own mother had followed by dying her hair with henna; as a result, a dark red color now took the place of the usual black and the interloper gray. She noticed Kawthar smiling as she stared at her.

"This is your grandmother's legacy, my girl!" she said with a solemnity that was intended to suppress her own feelings of bashfulness.

Saniya was very proud of herself, of her common sense, and her program of reading. When it came to understanding the various dimensions of contemporary life, she placed herself on a higher plane than either Muhammad or Munira with all their education. And that was quite apart from the innate gift she already possessed for dreaming and surmise, of which God had left both the others bereft. Even so, she hated the idea of old age and its manifestations. Her goal was a never-ending youth, a thought that she blended with a pure love of life and God who was the Creator of all.

During their Friday lunches she noticed that Muhammad and Munira were both preparing their sons for careers in medicine and engineering. That made her worry about her beloved grandchild, Rashad, and what he might be able to achieve in his own future. She also kept a close watch on the developing beauty of Siham, Muhammad's daughter. She viewed it as an obvious pivot around which Rashad, Amin, and Ali would all be revolving. Such beauty would inevitably succeed in creating still more emotional problems for this family of hers which had always been beset when it came to matters of the heart. She prayed to God to keep things peaceful; it grieved her to think that God would probably have called her away before any of her grandchildren fell in love with Siham.

Within the secure cordon of the family there were frank discussions between Muhammad and Suliman Bahgat. They would usually begin after the grandchildren had left to play in the garden or stroll along the quiet Helwan streets in the dry, clean air.

"These days," said Muhammad ruefully, "a father can't even speak his mind in front of his own son!"

"But there are millions of poor people who don't know what fear is!" Suliman replied, as Munira chuckled quietly to herself. "This is the era for poor folk."

"It's even better than that," Muhammad went on. "It's the era for poor and rich alike. God is indeed the creator of all, and for every human being He arranges a good deed that is pleasing to Him!"

The new leadership established itself and proceeded from one peak to another until there arrived the magic moment when Syria and Egypt were united and became a single entity. Now the idea of Arab unity was turned into a concrete reality, one that had previously been simply a historical movement in the imagination of many. Those who supported it worshiped the concept, while its opponents simply acknowledged the reality of it, pointing out that this time it was no child of chance or foreign conspiracies, but rather the result of a solemn pledge aimed at changing the course of history. The citizenry turned into vultures and dinosaurs, while the new regime assumed gargantuan proportions. The heavens bestowed a soothing balm aimed at salving the wounds of a people who for centuries had been ground into the dirt by the stamping feet of oppression and enmity. However, as often happens in the history of nations, it was not long before happy people were forced to watch as, right out of the blue, a meteor came crashing down on this unity and, in a single devastating moment, smashed it into a thousand fragments.

What a shattering blow it was for everyone as they clustered around their radios in different locations! Everybody said exactly what was on their mind. Once again malicious and sarcastic voices were heard. Nasser, the new leader, greeted the blow angrily and channeled his fury in an entirely different direction. The result was the new socialist laws that exploded into people's midst. The poor people of Egypt now scored a historic victory as a result of a conflict in which they had not been involved in any way.

"Lawyers don't count anymore!" was Professor Abdel Qadir al-Qadri's comment to Muhammad.

He was in his forties and a member of parliament; back in the fifties he had been appointed to the senate. He was a powerful orator and a parliamentarian of note. But now he looked permanently pallid and grim, with his suitcase ready for the anticipated trip to prison.

Muhammad was well aware of the implications of the situation. "Life's going to get a lot tougher," he confided to Ulfat.

For the first time ever, Kawthar started to pay attention to things going on around her. The socialist laws did not affect her personally, but she could feel the gun pointing directly at the fortress to which her social group belonged.

"I wonder what the future holds for us?" she asked her mother.

"Whatever it is," her mother replied, "was predestined before God created heaven and earth!"

"I'm thinking about Rashad," Kawthar went on sympathetically, "and you as well."

"He is the Merciful, the Compassionate," her mother responded.

I wonder if the flood will overwhelm us, Saniya asked herself. Nasser's new laws were intended to benefit the poor who owned nothing, so Muhammad and Munira were both safe. With Kawthar on the other hand, things were different, and for Rashad as well. They both owned land, shares in apartment buildings, and liquid assets.

"An era that managed to do what it did to Muhammad," Kawthar commented anxiously, "is not going to spare an old woman."

Saniya started thinking and then thinking some more. Her dreams for the house and family grave had obviously receded several steps.

"You should take your funds out of the bank," Muhammad suggested to Kawthar one Friday at the family gathering, "and keep them yourself before the beast catches the scent."

"But any common thief could steal my money," was Kawthar's instantaneous reaction.

"Use it to buy gold and oriental rugs!" he told her.

At this point Kawthar looked over at Suliman Bahgat, her sister's husband, as though to get the official version.

"Compromise is always the best course of action," he said.

She was inclined to accept his opinion, all the while praying to God that He would keep Rashad's money safe.

"No one's safe anymore!" was Muhammad's comment as they all drove home in Suliman Bahgat's Fiat.

Munira kept her thoughts to herself so as to avoid annoying him: "But ninety percent of the populace is bursting with hope!"

"It's sheer piracy, that's what it is!" Muhammad went on. "Otherwise how come they're all living like kings?"

"Even in Russia that's the way the rulers live," said Suliman Bahgat.

"God have mercy on Umar ibn al-Khattab!" was Muhammad's reply.

Saniya had a dream. In it she saw the old house gleaming new; fabric repaired, doors and stairs replaced, and new furniture. The bedrooms had retained their old oriental touches, but the reception rooms and dining room were all modern. The garden had been redone; the grass was green again, and orange, lime, and mango trees were flourishing once more, along with beds of flowers and roses. The long wall surrounding the house was completely covered in jasmine. She spotted Hamid Burhan, restored once again to full health and vigor, working in the garden. She felt very happy, but still had a question for the gardener: "Why haven't you planted any henna trees?"

She did not tell Kawthar about her dream; the timing did not seem right. When the radio announced the revolution in Yemen and Egypt's position on the matter, she soon forgot about it altogether. Immediately after the Yemeni revolution broke out, the family got together. They discussed the situation after lunch.

"Now it seems we're supposed to be trustees of every world revolution!" joked Muhammad.

"It's just a temporary diversion," Suliman Bahgat replied. "When it's over, Yemen will take Syria's place."

"But most of the Egyptian people are still barefoot!" Muhammad insisted.

"You can't deny that you folk were the very first to get involved in the revolution against the Imam in Yemen!"

"When individual fighters choose to involve themselves, that's heroic," Muhammad responded. "But when it involves a state, that's an entirely different matter."

"I wonder what our dear mother has to say on the subject," asked Suliman Bahgat jokingly.

"My conscience objects to war," was her terse response.

"It's almost as though the Israelis made the decision!" scoffed Muhammad, commenting on the Egyptian army's involvement in the war.

But pretty soon Saniya found her mind preoccupied with something else. When she looked at both Munira and Suliman, she grew alarmed: why was it that Munira had aged so quickly, while her husband still looked as young and vigorous as ever? She was still several years shy of forty, but her magical beauty was fading unnaturally fast. Maybe she was not well; her heart never told her wrong. To outward appearances everything about Munira's life seemed fine: Amin and Ali were doing very well in primary school; in his job her husband was making much more than he deserved; she herself had been appointed an inspector without having to spend time in the provinces, all thanks to her brother-in-law. In spite of all that, the gap in age between her husband and herself seemed to be widening for no particular reason. As for Muhammad, he had learned to deal with his handicaps and the reduction in his salary, but made his own way through life wrapped in an unshakeable faith. His wife seemed quite content. When Munira's gaze met her mother's, she could read a very long page of questions and got the impression that her mother had uncovered something that she was trying to keep to herself. Were her own eyes revealing her secret fears, Munira wondered? The truth of the matter was that Munira had indeed noticed an undesirable change in Suliman's feelings and behavior toward her.

"I haven't married just one man," she told herself once when she was alone, "but a whole cluster of them!" But then she went on to put things into a context she knew, "But maybe that's what eventually happens to love!"

She could recall various words and situations she had come across during the course of her life in works on psychology, novels, plays, and films. Even so, she hated the very idea of revealing her misgivings to her mother. One day Suliman himself decided to change the subject.

"At last we've decided to bring a television into our home!" he announced.

Munira actually wanted to wait a while so that they could find out what kind of effect it would have on the children. Muhammad and Kawthar were of the same opinion, but Suliman did not agree.

"We can't live outside the bounds of our own times," he said.

In fact Munira agreed with him deep down, so she soon gave way on the matter.

"Television, Mama," said Rashad as soon as the visitors had left.

Muhammad soon followed suit, and the delight that the grandchildren showed exceeded all expectations. Television brought favorite stars and the entire world to them where they sat, not to mention their revered president who shared time with them night after night. When Saniya first saw the television, she recalled the way the radio had made its first appearance in her house, when her mother was still alive.

"The day of reckoning will soon be with us!" was her comment.

In those times long ago there had been an almost total quiet on the streets of Helwan, so much so that people could actually listen to their own thoughts. But it was not like that anymore. Now the peace and quiet were continually being shattered by the din of apartments and even factories being put up. Even so, Saniya still felt completely content and relaxed. The entire country never slowed down; every day something new seemed to be happening, bringing both joy and sorrow. People's hearts were being split in two between the excitements of the present and nostalgia for the past. Their greatest fear was that the end would come before all their hopes had been realized.

"Now the whole world's going to be visiting us," said Saniya to Kawthar at the end of the first television transmission, "along with everything going on in it!"

Her daughter smiled, and then looked at Rashad. "We're not going to let anything get in the way of your homework, my dear," she said.

But the era of television had indeed arrived, and it caused a bitter struggle in the grandchildren's minds between school-work and watching television. Both Muhammad and Munira had libraries, and Shafiq, Siham, Amin, and Ali all used to like the children's books. Their interest had suggested that all would be well in the future; in particular they would do well next year when the time came to go to secondary school. But the advent of television showed that it was going to be a fearsome rival to reading. At first it only took up half their time, but it clearly threatened to take over completely. They were all approaching puberty, so they were naturally inclined to indulge in erratic and overt confrontations with their parents. During summer vacation they used to go out with their friends to squares, gardens, and cinemas. Quarrels would regularly break out. Each one of them demanded their own independence. There were very few things they agreed about, but the one thing that could produce total unanimity was the need to squat in front of the modern magic-box, with its infinite variety of programs and its welcoming arms that could envelop them from afternoon until after midnight.

Within this new adolescent war zone Rashad started to regard himself as the resident man of the old house and to find out details about his inherited wealth. In fact, due to his mother's weakness and the way his grandmother doted on him, things started to go from bad to worse. One Friday, Kawthar spotted him stealing a kiss from Siham in a corner of the garden. Withdrawing from the game the grandchildren were all playing, Siham returned to the house where her grandmother and parents were sitting. She looked flustered. Kawthar was afraid she was going to make a fuss about the way Rashad had treated her, but things passed without further comment. Once the other visitors had left, Kawthar confided to her mother about what had happened.

"Oh, that's just an innocent game!" Saniya muttered.

"Siham's very mature for her age," Kawthar commented. "Munira should be keeping her eyes open!"

She thought for a while. "Do you think I should warn him?" she asked her mother.

Saniya's answer was to yell for Rashad to come. Sitting him down beside her, she broached the subject head-on as usual. "A little bird has told me that you like your cousin, Siham!"

Rashad blushed. "I know who that little bird is," he replied boldly, staring straight at his mother.

"What is it you want with her?"

"To marry her one day," he replied even more boldly.

Saniya smiled.

"The proper choice has to be made at the right time," Kawthar told him.

He studiously ignored his mother. "Please do something about it, Grandma!" he said to Saniya.

The following Friday she stayed out of the usual arguments, waiting for the chance to make her request. The discussion focused on the Egyptian "excursion" to Yemen, which had turned into a bloody nightmare, consuming both the blood of Egypt's young heroes and the money of the poor.

"Have you heard what they're saying about Umm Kulthum's famous song, 'To time [zaman] I'll consign you,'"

Muhammad joked. "Apparently the original of it is 'To Yemen [yaman] I'll consign you!!'"

"OK," said Suliman contemptuously, "crack whatever jokes you like at the expense of the blood of these young heroes!"

"But how can anyone think this makes sense," Muhammad asked in all seriousness, "when we've got an enemy like Israel on our borders?"

"We've the largest fighting force in the Middle East," said Suliman, who had high hopes of becoming a secretary of state at the Ministry of Agriculture.

"Yes," retorted Muhammad, "thanks to those Russian infidels!"

"We're just taking their weapons and their notion of justice. Their beliefs are none of our business."

At this point Saniya lost patience. "Calm down, Muhammad," she said, "and let me have Siham for Rashad!"

At first Muhammad did not realize what he was being asked, but, when he did, he forgot all about his argument.

"Good heavens," he said with barely disguised glee, "they're still children."

"But I'm being very serious,' his mother replied. "Rashad is a real prize."

"And so is Siham. But it would be ridiculous to announce an engagement now."

"Are you saying no?"

"Absolutely not. Let's recite the Fatiha over it. We can consider it a reservation to be taken up when the time's right. But I'll have to ask the girl first . . . ."

Everything was agreed, and the reservation was made. When it came to working, Rashad regarded his developing love for Siham as a primary focus, but overall it was swimming that was his principal interest. In the sports realm he was ahead of all his friends, but in politics and religion he was a moderate. In spite of his awareness of his own wealth and pedigree, he was kind and tolerant and liked people. At the same time he was very proud of his physical prowess and good looks. He dearly hoped that the family's "reservation" of Siham for him would manage to satisfy his feelings of love within the bounds of decorum. And yet, while Siham seemed to like him, she offered him no encouragement. Following her mother's advice, she no longer played with her cousins in the garden, choosing instead to sit with her grandmother and listen somewhat listlessly to the conversations about politics. If anyone made the slightest negative comment about the president, she felt angry, but even there the page was not completely blank. She would occasionally hear bits of suspect information from her girlfriends at school or at home, all of which provided a link between what she herself was hearing and some of the allusions that could be heard on the television. Since she regarded her mother as a friend, she plucked up her courage enough to share some of the jokes with her, a few of which had a distinctly sexual gist to them; all of which led Ulfat to suggest that she needed to choose her friends more carefully. And that led Ulfat to discuss the matter with Munira.

"This television is giving young girls the kind of information that used to be only available to mature teenagers!"

Munira was well aware of what she meant. Even so, her reaction was, "But isn't that better?"

"Yes, when it's for the good. But not the opposite!"

Munira thought for a while. "Maybe the latter case as well!" she said.

"Munira, you're a school inspector and teacher," said Ulfat. "But Muhammad thinks otherwise!"

"A building constructed on the basis of ignorance will never work!" Munira replied, then went on with a sigh, "With Amin and Ali the problem is that, as day follows day, they're forgetting how to read for enjoyment."

"I wonder," Ulfat asked, "would it have been better not to let television into our lives?"

"There's no point in making decisions that go against the natural flow of life. The issue is how to make things work so that progress brings the greatest benefit and the smallest loss. The fact of the matter is that we're doing far worse things to them in our schools than television is doing . . . ."

"True enough! Even in politics there's no balance to their sense of judgment. They all believe in the president and every single word he pronounces—no before and no after . . . ."

"Not a bad beginning for people of their age," commented Munira with suppressed glee.

Like her two children, she was a Nasserist through and through, and was very happy about it. If only she had been as happy in her private life as she was with the public one. Even supposing that indifference was a fatal disease that would gradually gnaw away at the bases of love, even supposing its effect were visible in Suliman's expressions of love, then why was it that the same effect was not happening to her love for him? Why did she persist in loving this man with so many faults that they could hardly be numbered? Furthermore, the agonies she was going through did not end at this point. She was nagged by the nasty premonition that she was about to lose him.

One Sunday Saniya was preoccupied with her sad musings about Munira, when Muhammad burst in at noontime. Her heart did a leap. He went into her green bedroom ahead of her and sat down in front of her in order to share some news.

"Mama," he said, "I have it from an unimpeachable source that Suliman Bahgat has married Zahiya, the belly dancer!"

Saniya's eyes widened behind her spectacles. It was very cold, so she was wearing a heavy brown dress and a blue corduroy wrap.

A heavy silence ensued. After it had lasted for a while, Muhammad told her that the information was certainly correct.

Was it her destiny to inherit disasters, Saniya wondered. How could this possibly happen to the family's jewel of a daughter?

"Bad news is never wrong," she said to break her own silence.

Is there no one in my family who is accident-free? she asked herself.

"It's all in God's hands," she said. "Carry on . . . ."

"She has to be told!"

"I'm the best one to give her bad news. Then what . . . ?"

"She'll ask for a divorce. But I'm totally against that . . . ."

"I agree with you. It's just a temporary whim of his. But we're going to need a truly spectacular level of conviction to persuade her . . . ."

"So be it!"

Munira was immediately called into the room. Saniya adopted her normal direct manner in confronting bad news.

"I've some bad news for you, Munira," she said.

It was just like death, arriving unexpectedly even though it is bound to happen sometime. There was nothing new about it apart from the public revelation of a secret, nagging suspicion. Even so, Munira turned livid with rage and put on a determined expression.

"Totally disgusting," she said, and then continued decisively, "This means divorce!"

Saniya covered her face with her hands and thought for a moment. "Take it slowly," she muttered hopefully.

"There's no need for delay or thought!" was the reply.

"It's not good to rush into such a fateful decision."

"It's the only solution, Mama,"

"I don't agree," Saniya sighed.

"It's inevitable."

"The same thing happened to me, but I never thought for a moment about . . . ."

"That was ages ago. The circumstances are totally different now. I'm a school inspector. How am I supposed to meet men and women who know that I'm married to a man with a second wife?!"

"It's just a whim on his part. Think of your home, your children, and your future."

Everyone ganged up on her, trying to persuade her to wait a while. What was amazing was that Suliman Bahgat managed to ride out the storm with a combination of self-confidence and apathy, in the process making full use of his exclusive right to divorce and totally forgetting his former love story with Munira.

"We all have to learn how to deal with things that happen every time the sun rises," was his comment.

"Do whatever you want," Munira replied in a fury, "but let me go . . . ."

"Heaven forbid!" he replied with a totally faked anxiety. "You're the foundation of the family. You're the mother of our children."

"Were you thinking of our children," she yelled furiously, "when you did what you did?"

"I'm going through a rough patch," he replied quietly. "You're a mighty intellect, but I have no intention of neglecting my family!"

Munira found herself on her own in her reaction. Not only that, but divorce was not her decision in any case.

"I can only hope," Muhammad eventually told her, "that you'll put off any final decision for a month!"

He gave her a way out that allowed her to cover up her sense of defeat. Suliman Bahgat went on a trip to Morocco to attend a pan-Arab agricultural conference. When he returned to Abbasiya, he discovered that Munira had turned her office into a library and bedroom. In one corner she had put a couch that could be converted into a bed whenever needed. He felt sure that she had decided not to pursue a divorce and was actually taking the necessary steps to carry her decision through. Deep down he was delighted and launched into a sudden display of generosity.

"You're just the way you are," he said, "the way you were when we first fell in love."

For her part she hated talking to him and could not stand the sight of him. Now she had to endure the most miserable days in her entire life. Her love was totally buried under mounds of hatred, jealousy, and a profound sense of betrayal. She plunged into a lengthy dialogue with her own feverish soul. She deserved much more than she had received in return for loving such a flippant man. Maybe he could be excused for falling in love with her at such an early age. Even when she had grown up, the veil still had not dropped from in front of her own eyes. To the contrary, their love had developed even further, and that was when the danger had become that much more severe. Love had made her overlook his obvious shortcomings and led her to accept him, even though he was simply a handsome monster, with no brains and no soul. What motivated him was greed and profit on the cheap. The love she had felt was the strongest witness against her, filling her heart without bringing with it the smallest drop of respect. Can it be true that our lives are dominated by a blind, illogical force that utterly despises whatever level of culture and civilization we have achieved? The whole notion is as shocking as it is a genuine reality. So then, she told herself, my own punishment is far less than I deserve.

"That dreadful woman's a gypsy," she muttered in a fit of self-torture. "She's no inspector or teacher!"

From now on then, let all notions of love be plucked out by the roots from a heart that has clearly gone astray. Let her be proud like her mother, and refuse to be a rival to a woman who was most certainly her inferior.

Umm Sayyid had read the dregs in her coffee cup. "After so much hardship," she said as she brought her failing eyes close to the grounds in the bottom, "release will come."

She went on to suggest a number of magic ruses and visits to certain shrines that were famous for their efficacy. Munira smiled, but said nothing.

"The only cure for such treachery," she told herself, "is rejection."

In any case she was now freed from any kind of uncontrollable panic. No longer did she need to do things she did not want to—clinging on to the last vestiges of her former beauty—by dieting heavily and wearing a lot of makeup. Now she could devote herself to her work and her two promising sons, while finding a lot of consolation in her brother, Muhammad, whose faith and resolve remained undaunted. The two boys, Amin and Ali, were certainly shocked by their parents' separation, but clearly did not realize the full dimensions of the tragedy. Unlike their mother, who served as their nurturer, guide, and friend, they still maintained a friendly, if superficial, relationship with their father as well.

"Papa's made a mistake," was Amin's comment to Ali.

"And he's made Mama angry . . . ." Ali replied.

Every time Zahiya appeared on television, they both scrutinized her with a mixture of curiosity and sheer hatred.

"Here's my father married for a second time," Amin told himself, "whereas I've lost Siham forever!"

Why should that be so? He was no less handsome than Rashad; in fact, he was taller and more intelligent. But Rashad was certainly richer. Maybe he, Amin, did not love Siham as much as Rashad did, but he still cursed Rashad, Siham, and everyone else as well.

"Mama," he said one day, "this revolution is too even-handed!"

Munira was astonished. "Is communism what you want?" she asked.

"What's communism?" he asked in turn.

"Atheism," she replied after a moment's pause for thought.

He fell silent. He had to acknowledge to himself that Siham was not worth enough to make him change his religious beliefs. Munira knew more about what he was going through than he imagined, so she was sad to realize that both of them—mother and son—were suffering from the same disease. She was on the verge of tears.

"The things we imagine when we're young," she told him somewhat cryptically, "change when we get older!"

When it came to Ali, he had started wandering around a fairly strange valley as soon as he had reached puberty. He developed a spontaneous passion for Mervat, the mother-in-law of his uncle, Muhammad. He had seen her from close up when she came to visit Ulfat, accompanied by her latest husband, Professor Hasan Alama. Ali was not bothered by the fact that by now she was close to sixty. Her chic appearance, her sweet voice, her golden hair, and her gorgeous complexion all dazzled him. In no time at all he had developed a very individualistic passion for her. She became the first woman in flesh and blood who found a place in his heart, one that had already been fascinated by all the female stars on television.

She had managed to bolster his self-esteem. "Good heavens," she had said as she shook his hand, "you're as tall as two men put together!"

All the grandchildren now entered secondary schools. Shafiq, Muhammad's son, Amin, and Ali all went into the science curriculum, while Siham and Rashad studied the liberal arts. Rashad started talking about the future, much influenced by his conversations with his fellow athletes. He was dreaming of the life of a country gentleman, but that particular dream was clearly blocked by something that the president had said, "Those who don't work won't eat." Since he was such a powerful leader, he could clearly stop any lazy landowners from getting what they needed to eat.

"I shall tend my land," he told his mother one day, "and raise cattle."

"Then you should be going to the Agriculture Faculty," his mother pointed out.

He thought for a while. "Maybe Military College would be a better idea."

All Kawthar could think of was the miseries caused by wars. "No, no," she said. "Don't expose yourself to so much danger!'

"Our lives are all in God's hands," he replied, looking at his grandmother.

Had he been able to look forward to a country gentleman's life, he would certainly have married Siham when he finished secondary school, if only to put an end to the ravenous hunger that kept piercing his flesh with honey-tipped daggers. These were times when the Friday family gatherings began to lose their youthful fervor. In fact, only Muhammad, Munira, and Ulfat came. Although no one was surprised that Suliman Bahgat no longer attended, he was not completely cut off. Siham would also come most of the time, but where were Shafiq, Amin, and Ali? Whenever Saniya asked that question, the response was always that they were traveling, at the cinema, visiting friends, and so on . . . .

"Don't they feel any affection for me anymore?" Saniya asked.

"Of course they do, Mama," Munira replied. "But the world has stolen them from us!"

Now a new friendship stole its way into Shafiq's heart, in the form of Aziz Safwat, a school chum of his. The boy's father was a simple worker in a commercial office. His general life and appearance were both exceedingly modest, but his conversation was very varied, a trait that reflected his regular visits to the Egyptian National Library. All this made Shafiq very enthusiastic and Siham as well. Sometimes Ulfat used to follow their conversation.

"That friend of yours doesn't like anything!" she told Shafiq.

His father, Muhammad's, reaction was even less positive. "I don't like this type of individual," he said, "nor do I approve of mingling with other classes. But I'm only offering advice, not imposing any kind of injunction. No intelligent person refuses to accept an opinion until he's tested it."

Both Shafiq and Siham had long since learned what their own father thought of this particular era, as did Amin and Ali.

"Islam should be both the support and goal," he was finally able to say to Shafiq.

"I'm a Muslim, Papa," said Shafiq, "but I'm a Nasserist as well!"

Aziz Safwat was not against Nasserism, but he was not Nasserist enough to satisfy either Shafiq or Siham. Whenever the two boys were alone together in a café, the topic of women was their primary focus of attention; they both spent most of their time eyeing girls.

"I live in Bulaq," said Aziz. "It's a popular quarter with lots of good opportunities."

"Getting to meet girls is a terrible problem," commented Shafiq. "There's no easy solution!"

Aziz sat there in his old trousers and cheap gray shirt. "What we need," he joked, "is either a car or a private apartment!"

Shafiq's imagination took flight as he recalled the faces of all the women in the building in Bab al-Luq. His adolescent passions kept lashing him and hauling him over coals. On one occasion he had spotted his cousin, Amin, in Tahrir Square walking with a girl about his same age; they were strolling toward an ice-cream stand. He gazed at them enviously. Amin seemed very happy with his female companion, who looked very short alongside him. She was svelte and had a lovely olive complexion. Amin had noticed that she lived nearby and kept hanging around her every day at the tram stop. Then she had given him a little smile of encouragement, and they got to know each other, meeting regularly and exchanging kisses whenever possible. They became lovers. He learned that her name was Hind Rashwan, daughter of a mechanic who worked in a car repair shop. Like him she was at secondary school, the oldest of four daughters; the other three were still in primary school. This information did not exactly thrill him, but he managed to move beyond it; in any case, his ambition never flagged. After all, he was competing in an atmosphere in which every member of the 'elite' was doing his best to establish his popular origins as a way of avoiding the social upheavals caused by the new regime.

Ali on the other hand continued to enjoy all on his own—and in complete secrecy—his love for Mervat Hanem. He realized, of course, that she had also been his grandfather, Hamid Burhan's, wife, but that did not put him off. His passion kept him partitioned off inside his own pastimes, like television and a love of solitude. What encouraged both boys was a similarity to Munira in the way they dealt with life. Like the two of them, she too wanted a share of the era in which they were living, a posture that was diametrically opposite to the views of their aunt Kawthar and uncle Muhammad who regarded them all as if through an aperture from some unknown time in the past. By contrast, they were children both of present and future. For them the past meant nothing. They were citizens of a mighty country that now dominated not only the Arabs but Africa as well, the ally of one great power and imminent threat to another! Their immediate problems revolved around matters of sex, all of which would eventually be resolved.

On the radio an announcer's voice was heard mourning the passage of a major figure from the past, someone whom the younger generation had never heard of and a minority of people regarded as a traitor: the person in question was Mustafa al-Nahhas. The news had no effect whatsoever on the grandchildren. For a few moments, Kawthar's and Munira's eyes widened, but then they too simply carried on with what they were doing.

Saniya was walking from the living room to the veranda in the scorching August heat. Sitting on the closest chair, she stared sadly at the neglected garden.

"Ah well," she muttered to herself, "every age has its own book, as the saying goes. We commit him to God's mercy and good favor!"

Her own intimate recollections brought with them a profound sorrow. For Muhammad, it all made a vein in his forehead throb; he saw past, present, and future all clustered in a single gray tableau exuding both grief and mercy. At the time he was sitting in Professor Abdel Qadir al-Qadri's room. He watched as the old man leaned on the chair-arm, placed his hands on either side of his face, and fell silent for a while. He then humbly recited a verse of poetry:

> Ah me! Make a fine display of angst, my soul;
> That whereof you cautioned has now come to pass.

"The last great leader has died," he went on, staring morosely at Muhammad.

Muhammad did not comment, preferring simply to share the professor's grim mood.

"The funeral tomorrow won't even be worthy of a fourth-rate belly dancer," Abdel Qadir al-Qadri said.

But quite unexpectedly the funeral turned out to be an enormous explosion of sentiment. Muhammad watched the whole thing from a balcony on Sabri Abu Alam Street.

"Why has this fairy tale come to pass?" he wondered, hardly believing his eyes.

A never-ending flood of people, heartfelt slogans flying through the air, copious tears flowing, men young and old alike showing signs of genuine grief—yes indeed, young folks as well!

"Where did all these young people come from?" Muhammad asked himself.

How could this representative of the *ancien régime* have managed to exert such a pull on people at the very hour of farewell when, to all appearances, he seemed to have vanished from sight and hearing long since, duly suppressed by informers and shrouded in a layer of oblivion? Did the Wafd still have this huge number of supporters? Was it really the case that everyone who loved freedom but was now deprived of it belonged to the party? The entire crowd of mourners was participating in a corporate grief, both profound and intimate, as though bidding farewell to this world and its only hope.

In the crowd Muhammad spotted Professor Abdel Qadir al-Qadri. He was being buffeted by wave upon wave of people walking behind the coffin and gesturing enthusiastically. He never imagined that he was looking at his boss for the last time: that very same evening the professor was thrown into prison along with the more spirited mourners. He spent two years in jail and died just two days after being released.

At the family gathering the following Friday the big funeral was the subject of a good deal of talk, but Muhammad had another piece of news to share which was no less significant.

"Your husband's building a villa in Maadi!" he told Munira.
His sister gave him an incredulous look.

"Where's he getting the money?" Saniya asked.

"He's renting out furnished apartments," Muhammad went
on, winking with his one eye. "Thanks to sequestration and his
brother, he's been able to rent them himself unfurnished." He
gave everyone a look, then continued, "So he rents the apartment
unfurnished, then arranges for the belly dancer to furnish them.
They're partners!"

"Half his monthly salary," sneered Munira. "That's all we'll
ever get out of him!"

"People say," Muhammad went on, "that his wife has close
ties to the secret police!"

One day they all became aware of the army parading through
the streets of Cairo. Munira, Amin, and Ali were able to watch the
entire, impressive spectacle from their apartment balcony in
Abbasiya. Shafiq and Aziz Safwat watched it too in Tahrir Square.
The news soon spread that the army was on its way to Sinai to put
a stop to Israeli threats to Syria. All of a sudden the prospect of
war loomed in people's minds as an imminent possibility. At the
old house in Helwan, Kawthar looked at Rashad as though beg-
ging him to abandon his intention to join the Military College.

"What's the point of all these wars?" she asked. "They're
becoming like seasonal festivals!"

Saniya did not say anything, recalling a dream she had had
but had not revealed to anyone else. She had seen a tomb
open, and the coffins arranged inside. She had been calling out
to someone, but her voice had not been heard. She was on the
point of mentioning this dream of hers, if only by allusion, but
changed her mind and said nothing.

"These days," Kawthar went on, "Helwan's turned into
nothing but war factories!"

"I wonder," asked Saniya, thinking of the old place, "could

72

our house withstand explosions from close up?" Even so, she went on, "But the president knows what he's doing."

Meanwhile in the apartment in Bab al-Luq, the talk was of war. The conversation involved Muhammad, Ulfat, Shafiq, Siham, and Aziz Safwat.

"What does it mean," asked Ulfat, "for the Straits of Tiran to be closed and United Nations forces withdrawn?"

"It means that, for the past ten years or since their supposed victory, Israeli ships have been passing through the straits with impunity."

But Aziz Safwat chose to ignore Muhammad's sarcastic response. "It means war," he said.

"And our army is bogged down in Yemen," Muhammad commented.

"We're the most powerful force in the entire Middle East," said Aziz Safwat. "The president has obviously thought about his next move before making this one . . . ."

For the moment Muhammad chose to keep his anger in check.

"In his speeches he certainly manages to convey a sense of confidence and power," said Siham.

For just a moment Muhammad thought Siham might be talking about Aziz Safwat, but he soon realized she was referring to the president. With that he secretly cursed the three of them.

In Abbasiya Amin noticed how worried his mother was.

"We're strong, Mama," he told her.

"I'm sure of that," said Munira, "but that's not what scares me. Israel isn't a problem. But if we decide to invade its borders, we're going to find ourselves confronting the United States . . . ."

"But the Soviet Union's on our side," Ali chimed in.

"And do you suppose it's going to destroy the entire world just for our sake?!" she asked.

"Nor will the United States destroy it for Israel's sake!" was Ali's retort.

"To tell the truth," admitted Munira, "I'm scared to death . . . ."

Suliman Bahgat called in to see them on an emergency visit. He would usually come by once in a while, and his relationship with his two sons was cordial, if somewhat negative. For her part Munira treated him in an officious manner. He listened to their various thoughts about the possibility of war, and then gave them the benefit of his opinions as though he had some inside information.

"There's absolutely no cause for alarm," he told them. "In my view there won't be a war . . . ." He paused for a few moments, and then went on, "But just to make absolutely sure, I'd like you all to move to Zamalek. It's safer than Abbasiya."

"Thank you very much," Munira replied coldly. "But we're not going to leave our home. We don't think it's necessary."

He was not going to annoy her by insisting on it; in fact he may well have assumed from the outset that she would not agree.

"People's spirits are very high," he said.

"Aren't we the most powerful fighting force in the Near East?" Amin asked his father.

"That's a given," he replied confidently. "But in any case I'm not anticipating a war."

Things turned out differently. At nine o'clock on the morning of Monday June 5th, 1967, the air-raid sirens went off, and what happened happened. In Cairo everything seemed quiet, apart, that is, from the crowds of people who clustered around radios as they broadcast news of tremendous victories for the nation. Munira followed the news as well, and her sense of alarm grew even more intense.

"Why aren't we hearing about any defeats?" she wondered.

Muhammad tuned the radio to the BBC and Voice of America. All of a sudden they were both side-swiped by entirely different information.

"What's going on?" Ulfat asked. "Do you believe this?"

"I totally believe that this is what's actually happening," Muhammad said, as conflicting emotions battled inside him. "The whole thing was just a paper construction built on corruption and unbelief!"

Eventually it was announced that the president was going to address the people. Old folks stayed in their houses, while the younger generation spread out across the streets and in cafés. Everyone waited for the speech with bated breath. They were all beset by conflicting emotions, their vision barred against the slightest glimmer of hope. Wasn't there supposed to be a direct linkage between what the president had to say and hope? Yes indeed, he only ever addressed the people when he had bouquets of encouraging and hopeful information to impart. But on this particular evening he spoke to them in a new guise, and with a completely different voice and spirit. One man became extinct, and another took his place, one who had to speak about a "setback." He was announcing a general bankruptcy of ideas, ruing what fate had decreed, and bowing his mighty head to a crushing reality that had been stripped of all hope and pride. Now he was looking for a truly dismal exit strategy, surrendering his lofty position to a successor who would be forced to take over his own legacy, along with its heavy burden of absurdity and disgrace.

The brutal truth of it all now ripped people's hearts in two and hurled them into the very depths of despair. Tears from wounds buried deep down now rose to people's eyes. Saniya burst into tears, and so did Kawthar. Ulfat and Siham both cried, while Muhammad turned to stone. Munira cried for a long time. Shafiq, Amin, Ali, and Aziz were among the masses of people who poured angrily into the streets, yelling and screaming in anger as they made their way through the darkness. The noise they made was loud enough to drown out the buzzing of aircraft and the booms of anti-aircraft guns. They were all demanding that the president withdraw his resignation.

The days that followed were filled with feverish and crazy reactions: tensions, brawls, arrests, and suicides. The president remained in his position, but the army commander committed suicide. People stopped listening to political news so they could all open their hearts to a new and rare form of historical vision. They all began to participate in a comprehensive and totally modern form of exorcism; and they all did it with an almost masochistic pleasure. What had happened? How had it happened? Why had it happened? The whole public atmosphere bore witness to a veritable hailstorm of rumors, gibes, jokes, and tall tales, not to mention pools of tears. Symptoms of an unknown disease began to appear as well, one that to all appearances had no known cure.

The family gathering on the following Friday saw all the generations together at the old house for the first time in ages. The older folks looked sad, while the younger ones seemed stunned and totally at a loss. Saniya felt sorry not only for herself, but for her sons and grandchildren as well. She thought about her long-lost dream, about Hamid Burhan and the minor crusade he had lived by. She gave Muhammad a sympathetic look, and then stared affectionately at her grandchildren. She forced herself to listen to a little voice inside her that suggested that she forget all about her plans to refurbish the house and garden. Who on earth could be thinking about such trifles now that everyone was being roasted in such a fiery hell?

"How sad it all is!" she muttered.

"The problem," said Muhammad angrily, "is that we've forgotten about God, so he's forgotten about us!"

Suliman Bahgat, who was sitting there like a body with no soul to it, had a different view. "The whole thing's the result of American treachery!"

"There's no excuse for negligence and stupidity!" yelled Muhammad. After an angry sigh, he went on, "And what do people do? They all stick with him instead of demanding that he be put on trial!"

He stared hard at his son, Shafiq. "What on earth possessed you to join the rest of the mob?" he asked.

"I don't exactly know," Shafiq replied. "Maybe I had the idea that life cannot go on without him."

"What we told ourselves," Amin interjected, "is that the enemy was keen to get rid of him, so we all stuck with him as a way of confronting the enemy's decision."

Muhammad gave a sarcastic laugh. "Do you really think the enemy is keen to see someone better than him in power?!"

For a few moments Muhammad said nothing, but then he continued. "I'll confess that I too am happy that he's stayed on. Yes indeed! Now he has to remain at the top of the rubbish heap that he's created. Let him suffer along with everyone else and assume the burden of putting things right. That's better than fleeing abroad somewhere and enjoying a millionaire's life!"

Shafiq, Siham, Amin, Ali, and Rashad all stayed quiet. It was almost as if the entire thing no longer involved them, or as if their Nasserism had drowned in a swamp of total despair. Now they had to wade their way silently in the dark. Meanwhile Suliman Bahgat said nothing for a while. Eventually, however, he gave them something fresh to think about.

"There's talk about reforming the army along new lines."

Muhammad guffawed yet again. "We're just a time zone that's beholden to the Soviet Union," he said. "It's not just Israel and the United States that are the victors. The Soviet Union has won too. Today its cronies have the nerve to tell us that socialism is more important than Sinai!"

"We still have God," Saniya muttered sadly.

"Is this the way things are going to end up?" asked Siham.

"Of course not!" replied Suliman Bahgat, assuming that the question was one to which he should respond. "We'll find that this is an opportunity to take another look at our own situation. Corrupt elements have managed to bore their way into our very bones. Some people even say the president was one of its victims."

"But he himself said he was responsible," Muhammad commented angrily. "That may have been the first time in his life he's ever told the truth!"

At this point Suliman Bahgat began to lose some of his composure.

"Enemies of the regime are gloating for all they're worth," he said. "It's almost as though this disaster happened to another nation, not ours."

"They're sad, not gloating," replied Muhammad, waving his arm in objection. "The previous generation tried its very best to set a time limit to the British occupation of Egypt, then along came a set of heroes who dreamed of creating an empire. Their efforts resulted in the importation of a new occupation, one that was put into practice by Israel, the smallest and newest state in the world, it being the inevitable consequence of ignorance, delusion, corruption, and tyranny. When you look at people today, the only ones who seem balanced and settled are the communists!"

"But we aren't communists at any rate!"

"No, but you're all hanging onto their coattails."

"If you'd devoted to fighting Israel a mere tenth of the energy you've used to fight Muslims in Egypt, you'd have won!"

"The struggling masses are instinctively aware of the direction they need to take," Suliman said testily.

Muhammad now lost his sense of perspective. "Don't talk to me about struggling masses," he said. "What about furnished apartments?"

Suliman blanched, and his expression suggested that things were going to turn nasty. With that Saniya intervened.

"No, no," she insisted. "I won't allow this. We're all family here, and there's no cause for fighting . . . ."

A general gloom now descended over the entire group. Suliman Bahgat no longer made an appearance at the old house, not because of his argument with Muhammad, but rather because one of the people investigated after the June war was his wife, the dancer Zahiya. It was determined that, through her contacts in the secret police, she had exploited her influence to make illegal profits. As a result, she was sentenced to five years in prison. Not only that, but the corruption purge also identified Suliman's officer brother who was also put in prison. Suliman now found himself alone and weak, with no support, and dogged by an evil reputation, all of which forced him to resign his post. He now stopped further construction at the villa in Maadi and lived in it by himself until Zahiya came back. All of which provided nourishment for Saniya's wounded heart. She imagined that these events might lead to Munira and Suliman renewing their old relationship. But Munira squelched that idea.

"I've completely finished with him," she told her mother.

Suliman was of the same mind. Munira was still devoting her entire life to her job and her two sons. By now she had already been promoted to inspector and took life even more seriously than before. One year she joined Muhammad in making the pilgrimage to Mecca, after which she imitated Kawthar by observing all the necessary rituals of the faith, although, in doing so, she was following the pattern set by her mother rather than Muhammad. But she still stuck to her Nasserist loyalties, although that was more an emotional reaction than an intellectual one. She too rejected the idea that he needed to go.

"He's simply the victim of worldwide imperialism," she said.

Middle age started to creep up on her, even more than it did on Kawthar. However, luckily for her, she did not notice the way her lovely face was changing to the extent that other people did. In any case, she stopped using make-up.

The student demonstrations were as much of a surprise to her as they were to many others. They were the first real internal challenge to the president, and from his most loyal supporters at that. There were calls for him to step down, and the atmosphere was loaded with sarcastic slogans. Everyone was eagerly waiting for the people to make up their minds; they needed to find out the real facts about the past. Munira found herself torn: on the one side were her sons demonstrating; on the other stood the president she so admired. The attitudes of both Amin and Ali amazed her just as much as those of Shafiq and Siham.

"But isn't he the president you went out on the streets to keep in power?" she asked, looking at her two sons.

"It's the people who have to play the primary role," Amin replied, repeating the ideas that were bursting in his mind.

"Do you want someone else to be president?"

"There isn't anybody else!" he replied with a shrug of his shoulders.

"So what's the point of holding an inquiry?" asked a perplexed Ali.

"Is it your plan to purge Nasserism as well?" she asked emphatically.

"We aren't being rejectionist," Amin told her, "but we're far from satisfied."

"You're all out of ideas!"

"We're totally confused," admitted Ali with a chuckle.

One after another they went to university. Two of them got what they wanted: Rashad went to Military College in spite of Kawthar's objections, and Siham went to the College of Arts, with the intention to study English. Both Shafiq and Amin had wanted to study medicine, but the admissions office consigned them to engineering. Ali wanted to go to engineering, but went instead to the College of Sciences. Once they were at university, they found themselves bombarded by an atmosphere full of loud and conflicting voices. Religion, religion, religion was one rallying cry; Israel only won because of the Torah, so our war had to use the Qur'an. Marxism, Marxism, Marxism was the next; only that could pull a really corrupt society out by its fairy-tale roots and construct a genuinely modern, scientifically based society on top of them. Then there was science, science, science; Israel's victory had been based on technology; our hopes for the future had to be based on science and technology. Democracy, democracy, democracy; it was tyranny that had done us all in. Nasserism, Nasserism, Nasserism; all we had to do now was be loyal to its principles in order to be loyal to our own country. The vortex of ideas kept spinning wildly, never stopping. People still had heavy hearts and bitter premonitions; the outlook was grim, desires were suppressed, and daydreams thwarted.

"We're an entire generation of victims," Shafiq suggested to his father one evening. "Whoever first said that, I believe him!"

"Victims of whom?" Muhammad asked.

"All our predecessors."

That made Muhammad angry. "And what do you know about Egypt before the revolution?" he asked.

"Let's forget about that," Shafiq said. "But what can you say when I want to be a doctor, and the government tells me to be an engineer?"

"I know your country," replied Muhammad in exasperation. "My library's at your disposal."

Shafiq now got to know his friend, Aziz Safwat, even better. He realized that he was a Marxist, something that had not occurred to him before, partially because he did not know enough about such things, but also because Aziz had always criticized a variety of issues without revealing his own political leanings. Now Shafiq noticed that the 1967 defeat did not affect Aziz even one tenth of the way it did other people. That brought to mind what his father had said, about how "balanced" the communists were. One day, as the two of them were strolling aimlessly around downtown, he gave Aziz a strange look.

"Might you be one of those people who actually prefers socialism to Sinai?" he asked.

Aziz's wan face broke into a smile. "The need to move toward socialism," he replied, "is the one genuine benefit of the July revolution."

"So you're a Marxist?" Shafiq said, staring at his friend in amazement.

Aziz started talking about the need to tear everything down and rebuild. The notion of chaos appealed to Shafiq and fired his perplexed soul. But Aziz kept treating sacrosanct entities with such unanticipated and withering sarcasm that, in spite of Shafiq's fairly wishy-washy sense of devotion, he felt an abrupt knee-jerk reaction against his friend. A strange mixture of stubbornness, anger, delight in argument, and rejection of extremism led him to argue with Aziz's opinions. It was almost as though he had a political posture of his own, whereas the only doctrine he knew about was Nasserism, the very thing that the 1967 defeat had just sent reeling.

"What I really need is a woman," he told Aziz when he had had enough arguing.

"I know of a great opportunity," Aziz replied with a laugh.

It turned out that Aziz had a girlfriend, and she had a sister who might suit his requirements. He got to know them both better; they were still schoolgirls and their mother was a poor widow who earned her living buying rotten fruit at rock-bottom prices and reselling it to the poor. She had not stinted when it came to educating the girls, but, even so, they had both decided on their own that they were going to continue whether their mother agreed or not.

"I've a furnished room on the roof," said Aziz Safwat. "The expenses aren't bad."

One day Shafiq accompanied Aziz to his roof apartment on Bihan Alley in Bulaq. He made his way through dingy alleys the like of which he had never seen in his life. He only started feeling comfortable breathing again once they got to the roof. Looking over some roofs toward the south, he could see the Nile River and the opposite bank with the trees, palaces, and apartment blocks in Zamalek.

Aziz took him to his apartment. Shafiq was shocked; it was just four meters long, and two wide. There was a couch to the left of the door and a tiny window on the opposite wall. A nail protruded from the right-hand wall, and the floor was covered with a brown rug. Shafiq frowned, but Aziz was not paying any attention. Soon Zakiya Muhammadayn arrived, wearing gray slacks and a blue shirt open at the neck. Her hair was parted in the middle; she had nice features and an attractive body. Aziz introduced the two of them, and Shafiq expressed his approval. With that Aziz departed.

Shafiq made love to her as only a starving, deprived soul can do. She chatted volubly and without restraint as though she were in her own home. Shafiq felt some pangs of regret, but he clutched her to his chest with a frenzy. For his part, the relationship continued its happy course, as though she could provide him with everything he desired. He still maintained his friendly relationship with Aziz, but that did not stop him from arguing with him whenever Aziz spoke ill of Islam. Yes indeed, he actually found himself defending Islam as though he was one of its advocates. He noticed something that troubled him: once in a while he could sometimes detect in his sister's expression a certain admiration for Aziz Safwat's opinions.

"Maybe you don't realize he's a Marxist?" he asked her one evening when they were alone together.

She gave him a blank stare but said nothing.

"Do you agree with his communist ideas then?" he asked.

"The problem is," she said after a pause, "that they're all new and exciting!"

"So have you given up on Nasserism?"

"I don't think so . . . ."

"Does Islam mean nothing to you anymore?"

"Inconceivable!" she said after a moment's thought.

"You've got no idea who or what you are!" he told her, as though describing himself.

Another surprise was just waiting to make itself known. Rashad had barely started strutting around in his uniform as a student at the Military College before he returned to another topic with his mother and grandmother.

"Now it's time to announce my engagement to Siham!"

Kawthar liked the idea, although she did not know why. In fact she wanted the wedding to take place as soon as possible. Saniya liked the idea too and told Muhammad and Ulfat about it.

But, when Ulfat raised the topic with Siham, she had another answer, "I'm sorry, but no!"

Ulfat, Muhammad, and Shafiq all looked at each other.

"Do you want to wait longer?" Ulfat asked.

"I don't want it at all!" Siham shot back.

Everyone looked stunned and exchanged disapproving glances.

"But you've been in agreement all this time!" said Muhammad.

"The whole thing was a joke," Siham replied with a quiet determination. "It's become clear to me that I can't possibly agree . . . ."

"But Rashad's a wonderful, wealthy, and good-looking young man," Ulfat shouted at her. "And he's your cousin. Just think about what will happen if you turn him down!"

"When you're talking about your own future," Siham responded with even greater determination, "anything is easier to bear than a sheer lie."

"I'm a believing Muslim," Muhammad sighed. "The believer believes in marriage among other things. If I had any money, I would see that Shafiq was married, and he's a man. But what about the woman?"

"But Papa," Siham sobbed, "I don't want to . . . ."

Now sympathy got the better of him. "It's all in God's hands," he sighed. "I'll give in, even though I hate the idea. I'm very unhappy, for myself, for you, for the future, and for everything around us. The earth's attraction has died, and everything's floating off into space!"

It was part of his temperament to deal with things head-on, so he immediately went out to Helwan, where he sat in the living room with his mother, Kawthar, and Rashad.

"I'm the bearer of bad news," he told them.

With that he told them the sad truth, placing himself right in the middle, like them, as a victim just as much as they were.

"We can no longer control our own children!" he said.

Their spirits all sank, as though each one had suffered a terrible blow. No one said a word. They all just sat there until Muhammad left.

Kawthar burst into tears. "My son's the best boy in the whole family!" she said.

"God will send you someone better than her," were Saniya's comforting words.

Rashad headed straight for the apartment in Bab al-Luq and asked to be alone with Siham.

"What's made you change your mind?" he asked her, "You've allowed me to love you and pin all my hopes for the future on you."

"I apologize for making such a mistake," she replied quietly. "I'm sorry. You're a wonderful young man, but there's nothing I can do about it . . . ."

That made him even more miserable. "Is there someone else?" he asked.

"No!" she replied tartly.

"Well," he said after a short silence, "if that's the case, why don't we give it a chance?"

"I'm sorry," she replied apologetically. "Just forget the whole thing and forgive me if you can . . . ."

"Is there someone else?" Muhammad asked Ulfat when they were alone.

"Certainly not," she replied. "She never keeps anything from me . . . ."

"That makes it even worse!" he shouted.

But there was "someone else." Siham made no mention of it because he had not revealed his feelings as yet. Maybe she was imagining things, but what was clear was that she felt a strong leaning toward Aziz Safwat. The looks he aimed in her direction spoke louder than any tongue possibly could. Things happened at a slow, steady pace until she managed to open her heart to real love; it was only then that she realized that this was something different, and not like the feelings she had previously had for Rashad. Rashad had been strong physically and good-looking, not to mention wealthy, whereas Aziz was skinny and pale; he looked plebeian and poor. But what attracted her was the gleam in his eyes, his seriousness, lively spirit, and obvious intelligence. Actually Aziz had for a moment or two occurred to Ulfat as a possibility, but she had almost immediately rejected the idea as being entirely unacceptable. He visited Shafiq a lot and saw Siham a lot; but it never crossed her mind to keep her daughter secluded in any way. Sometimes she would sit down with them, and so would Muhammad. And then, wasn't it Muhammad who had insisted that she go to university? He had made do with setting an example to them all in his daily life of what Islam should be, urging them to perform the required rituals of the faith, and, as far as possible, spend some time observing its traditional culture. Having projected such ideas, he left the rest to God.

Amin, Munira's son, may well have been the only member of the family who actually enjoyed Rashad's misery, because he too had fallen for Siham. He told himself that he now had a golden opportunity. Moving beyond his relationship with Hind Rashwan, he started spending more time at his uncle Muhammad's house and expressing his affection for Siham. But from the very first gestures he was well aware that she was offering him no encouragement whatsoever; and with that he gave up any further attempts.

"She's a carbon copy of Mervat Hanem," was his angry reflection.

He immediately regretted betraying his feelings toward Hind Rashwan and decided to correct his mistake by declaring his love for her and spending more time in her company. In fact he did embark upon a completely new phase in his relationship with her, one that was marked by a renewed seriousness and warmth. He started thinking about the future and the impediments which stood in the way of marriage: the different social classes of the two families, and the inevitably long wait before it could happen, not to mention the heavy expenses involved. That very thought reminded him that his father was actually rich, although he also bore in mind the existence of

Zahiya, the belly dancer, who was still serving her prison term and was reputed to be not merely his partner but the actual force behind his profiteering. Not only that, but his uncle's influence had vanished for good when he had gone to prison. When it came to his family's income, it was just about sufficient for a very ordinary kind of existence without the slightest trace of luxury.

How he longed to spend some time alone with Hind Rashwan so that he could release all the tension he was feeling, but the only thing he could manage was to steal the odd kiss or hug on the side streets in Abbasiya. There was a certain emotionalism about his public demeanor as well; of all the grandchildren he was the one who remained loyal to the ideas of Nasserism. He admired his mother too for sticking by the president. That may explain why he felt more sympathetic toward his grandmother's plight than did his brother Ali. Munira picked that up and favored him in her own mind; not only that, but, when she returned from the pilgrimage to Mecca, he decided to join her in her religious interests, although he preferred to imitate her approach and avoid that of his uncle Muhammad.

Muhammad noticed the way he had gone back to his Nasserist beliefs. "I don't understand you, Amin!" he said.

"I'm sorry," Amin replied, "but I can't forget the things he managed to achieve: the way he got rid of the monarchy, agricultural reform, nationalization of the economy, free education, and the gains made by workers and peasants. Defeat, corruption, tyranny, none of them can make me forget those achievements!"

Even though his enthusiasm was nothing like what it had been before, it was still quite different from his brother Ali. Ali had lost not just everything, but also himself with it. He was wracked by a sense of complete failure. The sources of all his dreams had dried up, and he was able to detect the whiff of hostility in the purest void and on lovely moonlit nights. In the old days he had decided to get a new cat when his beloved old one died. In the same way he now swore to God that, after the 1967 defeat, he was going to avoid all trends and political movements. From now on his only principle of action would be rejection.

All this made Munira very sad. "What are your dreams for the future?" she asked him once.

"If only I could find a job in a better country!" he replied nervily.

"You'd abandon your own country?" she asked disapprovingly.

"It can go to hell!" he said firmly.

"No one else in the family thinks that way!" she protested.

"What do you mean?" he scoffed. "We've an uncle and a stepmother in prison!"

It was at this time that Professor Hasan Alama, the last of Mervat Hanem's husbands, died. As Ali took part in the funeral ceremonies, his mind drifted toward his widow. His long-deprived heart did a flutter, and he started dreaming about the woman whose image had never left him since she had captured his heart in his uncle's house. Behind his secret desires there now grew a sense of reckless adventure. Since he was already indulging a certain licentious streak, his behavior now became uncharacteristically brazen. He started counting off the days until the fortieth day after the death, then the following Friday he headed for Helwan, making the trip in the evening to avoid being seen. He rang the doorbell of the apartment his grandfather Hamid Burhan had used first as a love nest and then for his married life. Mervat Hanem recognized him at once in his blue trousers and white shirt open at the neck to welcome spring's gentle breezes.

She was amazed, but managed to control her emotions. "Welcome," she said.

He followed her into the lounge, almost blinded by his emotions. "I've come to offer you my condolences," he said after sitting down. "It's a bit late, but . . . ."

She thanked him for his sentiments, all the while looking at him suspiciously. She was wearing a black dress that revealed her arms and a large portion of her legs as well. Nor had the mourning process prevented her from paying careful attention to her coiffure and make-up. As a result she still had a certain glow to her; indeed she may have looked younger than her years. But, when it came to the lines around her mouth and eyes, the gaze was not to be deceived. Even so, he preferred to accentuate the positive over the negative. She well remembered the way he had looked at her during more than one visit to Ulfat's house and had not the slightest doubt that this visit was not without its own particular purpose. Could that really be true, she wondered? What was she supposed to do with him? The very fact that she welcomed him and offered him some coffee implied that she was still leaving the door ajar so as to see what the unseen future might hold. For his part, he was determined not to go beyond preliminaries.

"You have exquisite taste," he remarked, looking around at the gold-painted salon.

"Just like your mother's set," she replied with a smile.

He had noticed a picture of Hamid Burhan on the wall, shrouded in a black veil. He had no idea what to say. For her part, Mervat did not wish to make his sense of hurt any worse.

"Have you visited your grandmother?" she asked him.

"No, I haven't," he mumbled.

"Someone may have spotted you coming here?"

"No, there's not enough light on the street for that."

"In any case, I'm very grateful to you for coming."

With that he stood up to leave. "Would you mind if I came to see you when circumstances permit?" he asked.

"You don't even need to ask," she replied smiling. "Treat this as your home . . . ."

On his way back from Helwan, he told himself that she was a clever woman, so there was nothing to worry about on her account. After this visit he was preoccupied with a general examination at the college. However, once that was out of the way, he could look forward to summer vacation. Without pausing for a moment, he went out on a limb and paid her another visit.

"My college exams prevented me from coming to see you," he told her.

The visit was something that he had to do; no argument about it.

"Are you always on your own?" he asked, staring at her greedily.

"Almost," she replied sadly.

His expressions betrayed his desires with a force that brooked no argument. She understands me, he told himself, and she's just waiting. And, even if I have things wrong, I won't be losing any more than I've already lost. When she brought him a glass of lemon juice, he stretched out his hand and held her arm. She gave him a questioning look, so he drew her forcibly toward him and clasped his arms around her.

"Are you in your right mind?" she asked him, as though to protest.

"I haven't totally lost it . . . yet," he replied, standing up to his full height.

Thus did Mervat Hanem set out on her last love affair. That night recorded the very first word on its rosy page. Ali thereby saw an old and desperate dream of his duly fulfilled, while Mervat offered on its altar her own form of affection, brimming with life and memories of youth. The amazing thing is that he was as happy as she was, or even more so. Even more amazing was that she had an even stronger hold over him than he did over her. Through a blend of pride, generosity, and, yes, craziness, she managed to bolster his self-esteem, so much so that for him she became the one and only haven in life, one where he rediscovered his own self, a cure for his malaise, and a desire to carry on with his life.

At the same time Siham was pursuing a different track. The eager and ambitious side of her was enraged when she found out that Aziz Safwat would have to put an end to his studies when he finished secondary school so that he could earn a living working as a correspondent for an Arabic newspaper. By now, Aziz had given up trying to bring Shafiq around to his own political point of view. Indeed, even though he did not realize it at the time, he actually managed to convince Shafiq to turn more religious; as a result, Shafiq became just like his father. However, he had a totally unanticipated success in persuading Siham, something he had not even bothered about at first. Once that became clear, however, he decided to concentrate on her, heart and soul, until she became his entire purpose in life. He used to visit her at college and invite her on dates where they were alone together (in other words, without Shafiq). When she agreed to come, he reckoned himself duly blessed; he used to discuss things with her as a novice, but, when it came to emotional matters, he was unable to restrain himself.

"I've loved you all along," he told her, "maybe from the first time I saw you . . . ."

Her silence, heavy with hints of happiness, seemed to him even more significant than any intellectual discussions they might be having. Perhaps, he told himself, this response of hers is the real thing, something with a truly solid foundation.

"I'm sorry you have to stop your studies," she said.

"Does university give you anything it would be a shame to miss?" he asked contemptuously.

"I shall never give up culture," he went on, squeezing her hand.

He wondered what concerns she had about the future. He could envisage her in a gleaming light and admitted to her that there were issues, such as the university degree, differences in family status, and poverty.

"None of that bothers me," she said.

"No, they are real issues," he told her, "but only in a world that believes in such things. But, if we disavow such principles, then those issues disappear . . . ."

Her new love story made her feel eager to put an end to the world that was so antagonistic to her new beliefs, and yet she continued to waver on the brink. She sensed that she needed to feel more secure before confirming her adherence to this new reality. The family atmosphere in which she had grown up had inured her to telling the truth and saying exactly what she thought. But now she decided to lower a veil over her new situation. That was especially important in view of her father's beliefs, let alone her brother's, who had decided to ally himself with his father after failing to find any alternative source of conviction.

"I'll postpone the confrontation until the right moment," was the way she convinced herself.

Even so she could not forecast what might happen in the future.

"Do you have a clear vision of the future?" she asked Aziz one day as they were sitting together at the Genevoise.

"When you've decided to stop worrying about those things," he replied quietly with a certain touch of annoyance, "then I'll know you've finally arrived!'

She set out to gain his confidence, no matter what the

aggravations involved. For his part he had been using Zinat Muhammadayn, the sister of Zakiya, Shafiq's girlfriend, as an outlet for all the tensions his youthful self was feeling as part of the process of relishing the pure love he felt for Siham. But then came the day when Zinat unleashed a bombshell.

"I'm going to marry a Libyan businessman," she said, "and move to Libya with him."

"He'll put you in the trade there!" he responded before he had time to recover from the shock.

"I'll make more money there than here," she said matter-of-factly.

So she vanished from his life and left behind a nervous wreck, buffeted by the winds of chance. Meanwhile Shafiq and Zakiya had the roof apartment to themselves. She enrolled in the College of Commerce. Their relationship developed, founded on a feeling of companionship and a fair amount of mutual respect. All of which led Aziz Safwat to discuss the situation with Shafiq.

"This isn't a passing fancy anymore," he said, "at least not from your side of things . . . ."

"Shouldn't we worry that she'll join her sister at some point?" Shafiq asked with a smile.

"Quite likely."

"We're all in a state of collapse, just like our public institutions!"

"They're preparing for war,"

"Are we really going to embark on such folly?" Shafiq asked anxiously.

Aziz smiled cryptically. "From the very first instant," he said confidently, as though he himself were a member of the war council, "the Israeli air force will start bombing water, electricity, and transport facilities. That'll leave the task of purging the regime to the millions who live in Cairo!"

"So why on earth are we spending millions of pounds?" Shafiq asked disconsolately.

"We've no say in the matter!"

"What's the solution?"

"That's to be found within," replied Aziz with a smile.

"The truth of the matter is," Shafiq interjected angrily, "that the Russians occupied Egypt long before the Israelis!"

"The Israelis take things away," replied Aziz with a frown. "The Russians give. If it weren't for them, everything would be over by now!"

Shafiq felt a bitter taste in his mouth, but said nothing. "It would be a real disaster," he said, as though talking to himself, "if Zakiya decided to join her sister!"

Rashad Nuaman al-Rashidi, Kawthar's son, was ahead of them in joining the workforce. He enrolled in the artillery. Once he reached majority he received his inheritance—a fair amount of money.

"Let me have a chat with you," Kawthar said.

"I'm not going to get married the old way," he replied with a laugh.

"Marry the way you want," she replied eagerly.

The wound caused by Siham's rejection had yet to heal. "Be patient," he said, "there are no bridal candidates at the front."

That word "front" set her back; it was the first time she was hearing it. She looked over at Saniya.

"Everyone's there," he told her. "Our lives are in God's hands."

"Yes," Kawthar added grimly. "There are other words too, like 'deterrent' and 'attrition!'"

"My heart tells me everything will work out fine," Saniya said. "God will look after him."

She was putting on a display of fortitude as a way of supporting Kawthar. However she was actually churning inside. After all, Rashad was her favorite grandchild. Once she had finished her evening prayers, she started carrying out her intention to recite the Qur'anic Throne verse night after night as a way of conveying her own blessing to Rashad and all his fellow soldiers at the front. How long she had waited for him to achieve his majority so she could share with him her hopes for the old house, the garden, and the family tomb, but now here he was at the front! How on earth could her tongue convey her real desires in such circumstances? Whenever she tried to pick a rose, the thorns always got in her way. This was a family where sheer bad luck was never willing to proclaim a truce: Kawthar, Munira, Muhammad, Rashad, and Siham, all of them; and even before them there had been the tragedy of Hamid Burhan himself. So when, she asked herself, was divine providence finally going to start tending to their needs?

What was even more remarkable was that from now on she started devoting a whole lot of attention to her own person, as though to challenge the onward march of old age. She made a point of visiting clinics on a regular basis, quenching her thirst with the healthy mineral waters of Helwan, filling her lungs with the dry, fresh air of the town, and fending off the graying of old age with henna, a color with which she regularly tinted the crown of her head.

"When we're about to pray," she used to say whenever she noticed a smile on her children's faces, "we have to look our very best."

She often used to criticize Kawthar, Muhammad, and Munira for their indifference, since they all simply allowed old age to advertise the ongoing spread of its graying effects on their heads without putting up any resistance.

Then came the day when Umm Sayyid came back from the market with some surprising news. "I happened to spot Ali, Munira's son," she said, "slinking his way into Mervat's apartment building in the dark."

Saniya paused for a moment and frowned. "Maybe he was just visiting a friend," she said, and then mumbled to herself, "But he's never bothered to visit his grandmother!"

Next Friday she commented on it to Munira herself, and she in turn asked Ali about it after dinner one evening at her Abbasiya apartment.

"Did you really go to Mervat's apartment in Helwan the day before yesterday?" she asked.

His heart stopped; he felt sure he'd been found out. Without even realizing it, Munira rescued him.

"I'm not worried about the fact that you paid her a visit," she went on. "You may have actually been visiting a colleague, but surely you should have looked in on your own grandmother as well. You need to visit her and try to make her feel a bit happier!"

"I didn't have enough time!" he replied, swallowing hard. "In any case," he went on gruffly, "the old house is so boring!"

"Your grandmother's an amazing woman," she scolded him. "No way is she boring!"

He decided that he still needed to be careful, so he said nothing more.

When Rashad came home on leave, Cairo aroused all sorts of emotions in him: the eternal city living in a kind of time vacuum! From the very start he decided to talk frankly about life at the front.

"The front's not the way you imagine things to be," he told them after hugging everyone. "The things you hear are sheer exaggeration and fancy!"

He kept his own agonies buried deep inside him as a kind of holy secret, not to mention the shattering explosions, the bitter defeat that his generation had inherited from its predecessors, and the heavy burden of responsibility that they felt for what had happened, was happening, and would happen. That's why the situation at the front raised a whole series of general concerns, things that constituted an almost permanent framework to his entire way of life. In such a context Cairo seemed amazingly indifferent to it all; fractious and defiant even.

"Mama," he said without even bothering to ease into the topic, "I'm thinking of getting married!"

"I'm so happy to hear it!" Kawthar responded.

"No doubt, you've seen something to change your mind!" was Saniya's happy remark.

"This time," he replied cryptically, "things will come to fruition!"

The truth of the matter is that, during his nights of agonized suffering, the very thought of marriage had seemed like a shining inspiration. His determination had taken a leap forward when he had spotted the sister of one of his colleagues. It was not love at first sight; she was quite acceptable, and that was enough. He himself had not yet got over Siham, and he had spent his leave time hanging around with his colleagues. He visited his aunt and uncle as well and told them all the things he had kept hidden from his mother and grandmother. There, he discovered that Munira was more involved in public affairs than almost anyone else, and yet he still decided not to quench her thirst for more detailed information about the situation at the front.

"Cairo's so self-absorbed," Rashad commented angrily.

"What else do you expect?" asked Ali.

"People either declare war on each other or make peace," said Munira in exasperation. "But we've come up with a brand new kind of situation, one that has no precedents!"

In his uncle Muhammad's house, the tension in the conversation was several notches higher. When he set eyes on Siham, he felt sad and miserable all over again; the fact that she treated him with such a gentle reserve only made things that much worse.

"We all hope you'll be safe," she told him.

That did not make him feel any happier.

"Every single day," was how his uncle Muhammad chose to summarize his view of the situation, "he manages to sacrifice innocent lives, only in order to cover up his own faults!"

"Do you have a solution, Uncle?" he asked.

"There's only one solution," Muhammad replied. "The Islamic one."

For the first time, he got the impression that Shafiq was sympathetic to his father's position. He now realized how much the family had changed during his absence, between the time he went off to college and the time he had spent at the front. What he did not appreciate was how much Siham had changed. By this time, she had become a believer in total revolution. True enough, her heart had been the first agent of change, just as sheer stubbornness about personal philosophies had played a similar role with Shafiq. But the result was one and the same. Munira realized that she was engaged in a fierce struggle, and yet at the same time she had the impression that this was just the beginning.

Before she even knew it, Aziz Safwat was issuing an invitation. "Come over to my room, instead of hanging around somewhere else!"

She stared at the floor speechless, and her lovely face blushed. "Your room?!" she said.

"Suggestion hereby withdrawn!" he replied quickly.

What exactly did "withdrawn" imply, she wondered! The general idea delighted her, and yet she felt panic-stricken. To be sure she was always dragging along behind him, but for how long?

"So you're still you!" he told her affectionately. "Siham, darling daughter of the esteemed teacher, Munira Hamid Burhan!"

"No, no!" she replied. "Don't think badly of me. But it doesn't mean . . . ." And with that she stopped talking.

"It means that you haven't taken the next step yet."

"What's the hurry?" she asked. "There's nothing standing in our way!"

"So why wait then?"

Now he had her in a corner, since he had complete control of her heartstrings. When they next met, he treated her in a very odd way, but with complete self-confidence. They took a different route.

"We're going to Bulaq," he told her when she asked where they were going.

She went along with him like someone who had been drugged, all the while nursing the feeling that she was somehow crossing the borders of her own homeland forever. For his part, his heart was pounding with sincere hopes and the sweetest of intentions. As far as he was concerned, they were a single body and a single conscience. As they entered the almost furniture-less room, he stole a swift glance in her direction.

"It's certainly inferior to the kind of things you're used to," he said.

She looked out the window toward the Nile and shrugged her shoulders. He told himself that this room, with its own long history of infamy, was about to become, for the very first time, a haven of sincerity and genuine feelings. Even though Siham pretended to be feeling unruffled, her insides were actually churning with conflicting emotions. Her own desires were no less fervent than his, but it was not her desires that were making her submit to his will, or at least, not her desires alone. She had convinced herself that she was not in any way surrendering but rather rising up to some rare and unusual summit. However, in spite of that she was also worried that she might also be poised on the brink of an abyss of never-ending misery. Through inborn intuition of some kind she guessed that, in spite of his surface gruffness, he really needed her affection and that, for her part, she would be lacking the same kind of affection for evermore. She had already given a great deal without getting back anything to keep her intellect afire.

"Simply put," he said with a smile as he wiped his face, "this is marriage!"

That verdict, shrouded as it was in despair, annoyed her. Even so she gave him a smile.

"How do you feel?" he asked her.

"Happy," she replied, stroking his cheek.

"I admit that you are my good fortune in life . . . ."

"From now on," she went on hopefully, "maybe you won't be so resentful about everything!"

"That's simply the other aspect of profound happiness," he responded after a moment's thought.

This was the way Siham found herself reborn in an entirely new world, and she plunged into it for all she was worth. Actually she had no choice: it was either revolution or perdition. She was now finally separating herself from her father, mother, and brother. From this point on, she became a kind of fifth column in their midst. When she considered how far she had traveled from her times with Rashad to those with Aziz, the whole thing seemed like some kind of dream. Now every step she took was demolishing all that lay behind it, heading for an abyss that would never allow her to go back.

"The whole thing is very, very sad," she muttered to herself.

When would she be able to reveal her secrets, she wondered, without bothering about anything?

She redoubled her efforts in the educational sphere, simply out of a desire for more independence.

Meanwhile there was nothing new to relate about Rashad's marriage project. When the time came for his leave, he did not show up. Instead they received official word that he was being treated in the military hospital for a wound that was not serious.

Kawthar and Saniya both rushed to visit him in a state of indescribable panic. They discovered that his right collarbone had been hit by shrapnel and required some minor attention. Kawthar's state was even worse than Rashad's—he being the one who had been hit—even though his condition was not in any way alarming.

"I don't think you'll be going back to the front," she said.

"I'm going back as soon as I'm better," he replied with a laugh. "We're close to a truce," he went on, stroking her hand.

But Kawthar was convinced that they were still at war. "We were making plans for you to get married!" she said.

"It seems that my girl is already engaged!" he replied with a laugh.

"You could have any girl you want," she retorted angrily.

"You talk with all the confidence of a matchmaker," he said jokingly, "but you only ever leave the house when there's a disaster!"

However, it was Amin, Munira's son, who, totally unexpectedly, was the first one of his generation to embark on the path of marriage. He had noticed that Hind Rashwan was pursuing her business studies with considerable success. She told him quite frankly that she would like them to get engaged; she was fed up with keeping their relationship a secret. He himself was certainly in love with her, and agreed with what she was saying. He made his way into his mother's library where she used to spend some time every evening and sat down opposite her. She gave him a quizzical look.

"I want to get engaged!" he told her.

Munira was astonished and asked for more details.

"It's Hind Rashwan, our neighbor," he said simply.

He could sense at once that his mother was not happy; he had been expecting such a reaction from her. Even so, he knew she had plenty of common sense. His father would certainly

102

agree without hesitation, bearing in mind the example that he himself had already set.

"Are you sure?" his mother asked him.

"Absolutely, Mama," he replied. "She's a wonderful girl."

"Then so be it, with God's grace," she replied, keeping her inner turmoil to herself.

"Not to mention the fact that every family is supposed to be at least fifty percent workers and peasants!"

"But even the president himself has married his daughters to upper-class men!" she responded, revealing thereby a bit of what she was actually feeling.

In spite of a variety of previous relationships involving family members, this was the first genuinely joyous occasion for the entire family. People said that it was an engagement that fully reflected the peculiar era in which it occurred. The simple party was held in Hind's father's modest apartment, with Suliman Bahgat taking a leading role. Rashad found himself much affected by the ceremony, and his heart was filled with nostalgic affection. For her part Siham could feel to an extent greater than ever before how heavy the weight of the secret she was keeping was. Ali kept wondering why they had not invited Mervat, now his lover! All Shafiq could do was think of Zakiya Muhammadayn, assuring himself that she was no less significant than Hind Rashwan even though she belonged to a pariah class. From conversations with Hind's mother, Munira gathered that she was hoping that the couple would get married as soon as Hind graduated. That made Munira nervous; she wondered whether Amin was really ready for marriage. All her friends had similar concerns which managed to multiply like planets circling in their orbits.

But then all such concerns faded into insignificance when a totally unexpected tidal wave engulfed everything else; it felt just like an earthquake out of the blue. One evening the television programming changed abruptly; Qur'an recitation was the only thing available. Everyone was at a loss.

"One of our Arab guests must have died," was what some people said.

"It's not out of the question that King Hussein may have been assassinated . . . ."

But then on came Anwar Sadat to announce the death of the greatest of all Egyptians, Gamal Abdel Nasser. Here was the vice-president confronting the Egyptian people with the impossible as something that now had to be accepted as indeed possible. Everyone's heart missed a beat, and a totally new and fabled world occupied the space of what had gone before. When, how, why, everyone asked; could it be possible? But then, why not? No one ever imagined that they would witness his death, or even that he could die. For eighteen years he had been the driving force in everyone's heart, omnipresent, all-pervasive, a hovering presence in every single heart; both luck and boon, security and fear, hope and despair, friend and foe, power and weakness, yesterday, today, and tomorrow, peace and war, victory and defeat. If all these conflicting emotions were suddenly to disappear, what would be left?

The old house was shrouded in utter misery. Kawthar burst into the kind of tears that had no obvious logic behind them other than as a display of respect toward a very direct exposure to the realities of death, a feeling that was not without its share of fear and misgivings. Umm Sayyid and Umm Gaber both burst into tears, and, while Saniya remained silent for a while, her eyes soon teared up as well.

"His image will remain forever with us," she said.

Muhammad first heard the news while he was walking back to Bab al-Luq. One of his friends bumped into him and whispered into his ear. At first he didn't believe what he was hearing; he was scared that it was some kind of plot to get the president's enemies in jail.

104

"Don't go saying things you know nothing about!" he upbraided his colleague angrily.

"But I saw and heard the whole thing on the café television!" his friend replied confidently.

When Muhammad hurried back to his apartment, he discovered Ulfat, Shafiq, and Siham all gathered around the television, all of them teary-eyed.

"May he rest in peace!" he said.

As he sat down, he put his satchel in his lap and placed his cane against a table. Closing his eyes, he spent a few minutes in some other place until he came to himself again. Once he had recovered, he felt that he was living in some new kind of world; as though the chains around his neck, hands, and feet were being loosened. Suddenly he felt strangely light. Wafts of a new sense of well-being infiltrated his senses, and he soon succumbed to a feeling of profound joy. He was delighted, and there was nothing he could do to stop it, although he made every effort to keep it hidden behind his closed eyelids. As the sensation continued and even intensified, he secretly asked God to forgive him. He was scared the whole thing might get out of hand and make him faint.

When the full impact of death hit Ulfat, she burst into tears, the kind of crying she had never indulged in before. Shafiq and Siham joined her, linked as they were by emotional ties that had yet to dissipate.

"Who could have imagined such a thing?" Siham commented.

"He made us forget about everything," retorted Muhammad, "even fate itself."

"Who'll take over, I wonder?" Shafiq asked.

"Whoever it is can't be any worse," Muhammad replied sarcastically.

In the Abbasiya household Munira and Amin were just as miserable, the kind of misery that showed no signs of recovery any time soon, while Ali sat there totally stunned.

"There's no going back this time!" he said.

During those troubled times Aziz Safwat spent most of his time in the streets and in cafés; most of the time Siham was with him.

"Sadat will only be in for a short while," he said confidently. "The future belongs to our men!"

He too waded into the sea of universal sorrow, watching the funeral and listening to the broadcast on television. The tomb loomed like an inevitable act of closure; a cell plunged in deepest gloom. He imagined to himself the way the corpse would be laid in its final resting place, devoid of all glory, weighed down by a simple handful of dirt. All of a sudden he felt a totally unexpected sensation, which took the form of a whole flood of jokes—something that astonished him.

"He had a lot of enemies as well," Siham commented.

The whole thing seemed of a much broader scope than that. "He was a symbol of both love and fear," he said. "That's why it's entirely appropriate for his death to arouse very different emotions in people."

Indeed sorrow was not the only emotion that people were feeling. There was a surface level of sorrow, to be sure, but a suppressed joy as well and a nagging sense of fear, all of which played against each other in crazy harmony. Death was announcing in a loud voice that it had taken away Gamal Abdel Nasser himself. That made everyone aware of quite how close death always was; the same thing might happen to anyone without their even anticipating it.

"People are weeping for themselves first and foremost," he told Siham.

"They've grown used to watching him as the only actor on the stage, but now it's empty. Loss and panic, that's all there is to fill the void."

"I agree completely. In the past he wanted to step aside, but they forced him to stay on just like the revolution itself. But now death has freed him from their desperate grip and is forcing them all to take on a burden of trust, the kind of thing to which they have never become accustomed. That same desperation is making them all weep and crack inane jokes . . . ."

As time passed, the tempest gradually died down. But, before too long, the entire scenario witnessed a whole series of significant developments. Things reached a crisis point. The situation became more and more complicated, but the eventual result was unexpected. The new president managed to defeat his enemies convincingly. His victory suggested that an entirely new kind of leadership was coming into play; a fresh kind of populism was being born, one that was thirsty for victory and eager for security. As part of a quest for escape from accumulated crises, a brand-new phase now began.

By this time Rashad had returned to the front, fully restored to health; in fact, he seemed so involved in his job that for a while he forgot all about his project of getting married. However, Kawthar did not forget. But fresh concerns emerged when she started to have liver problems, to such a degree that, to the casual observer, she looked weaker than her own mother, who by this time was sixty but still retained her health and beauty. Both of them kept up a nonstop struggle against advancing age.

As autumn of that year drew to a close, it poured with rain. The roof over the lounge sprang a leak; chunks fell off the walls and drips came in through the eaves of the living room.

"We must have the roof repaired," said Saniya.

Kawthar agreed without hesitation. Umm Gaber the cook brought one of her relatives, who took off the broken tiles and replaced them with cement ones.

"Shouldn't we have the lounge and living room repainted?" Saniya asked.

Kawthar was well aware that her reserves were constantly in danger of running out. "No," she replied, "let's wait on that."

"Things are bound to get better under our new president," Saniya responded with a smile to hide her sense of defeat.

"But Mama," Kawthar went on gloomily, "Rashad's still stuck there at the front!"

"The president's still dealing with internal matters. He's been good at looking for a peaceful solution, and his relations with other Arab countries are improving day by day."

In the Bab al-Luq apartment, Muhammad had by now rediscovered the personality he had lost. For a long time he had resorted to clandestine chatter, but now he was talking openly. There were a number of meetings with old friends of his.

"The new president is a friend of ours," commented a friend one day in his office.

"But we have to rely on ourselves," Muhammad replied cautiously.

"Justice is on the march," the friend went on. "It'll even include the old feudalists themselves!"

He started reminding them of the failed experiences of the past. Shafiq agreed with him. Siham, however, had not been in favor of the new regime ever since Sadat had emerged as the winner. It was not simply a matter of repeating what Aziz Safwat was saying, but rather that she had by now reached the limit of her new intellectual development. Even the notion of religion had been ripped from her heart, and she felt completely alienated from her own family. When she was with them, she felt herself enveloped by a hidden threat of some kind.

"All this apartment needs," she told herself on one visit, "is a muezzin for it to turn into a mosque!"

She noticed that one of her teachers was fond of her, and the day came when he told her that he wanted to marry her. She was totally shocked and told him that she was already "involved." Needless to say, she was worried at the same time in case the information reached her family. For that very reason, whenever the subject of marriage was raised, she would always frame her response in terms of postponing things until the future: "I'm not even going to think about that until I've completed my studies." In her mind she framed a plan for the future, one that called for her to marry Aziz, even if it involved informing her parents by letter from somewhere else. As time went by, she learned to trust him even more and discovered his good qualities. Her innate sense told her that he really loved her, while he remained steadfastly loyal to his own principles. Even the anger he felt toward his enemies harbored within it a kind of romanticism dedicated to a humanistic vision that did not yet exist. He was someone who appreciated poetry and music, and loved dogs. However he hated the new president with a passion.

"He's a nasty, self-centered operator!" he said. "All he wants to do is to sidle up to Arab and western reactionaries!"

What made Siham even more anxious was the fact that her new political vision was no longer a carefully kept secret. In any number of conversations with her fellow students in the English department at the university the various comments she offered made her political stance clear enough. Not only that, but at least one of them had seen her in Giza with Aziz Safwat.

With Munira's family in Abbasiya, life carried on in relative peace, although Zahiya's release from prison aroused certain feelings.

"Aren't we obliged to visit the Maadi villa to offer our congratulations?!" Ali asked with a sneer.

However, by this time Munira had long since gotten over her love for Suliman Bahgat and had also reconciled herself to Abdel Nasser's death. She was totally preoccupied with her official position and private work in her library. With her graying hair and fading looks, she was the image of sedate middle age.

It almost looked as though she were the same age as her mother or even older. In fact, her mother scolded her about looking so old at such a young age, but she paid no attention.

Amin and Hind remained happily engaged, their life far removed from any incipient problems. Ali meanwhile continued to squeeze all the honey he could out of his continuing relationship with Mervat. Munira and Amin were still in something of a daze over Abdel Nasser's death, and their strong Nasserist sentiments were jolted when they heard occasional whispered criticisms of the late leader's period in power.

"What a nerve these people have!" she said in Amin's hearing.

"Don't be surprised," he responded angrily. "We're moving in a new direction!"

But how could they all get out of the basic underlying problem at the front? True enough, there was now a sense of security and the rule of law, not to mention the vague flirtation with democracy. But still the general atmosphere seemed sluggish, and the future was shrouded in dark clouds. People's nerves cracked, and demonstrations broke out at the university. Things reached a crisis point before calm was gradually restored. The grandchildren had very different opinions. Both Amin and Siham took part in the demonstrations, although for parallel but different reasons. Ali took part, but for no particular cause. Shafiq withdrew and joined the onlookers. One evening during the disturbances he came home to his family looking pale and distressed. He sat down in the living room.

"Aziz Safwat's been killed," he said, obviously distraught.

Siham let out a scream. "No, no!" she sobbed.

The family's reaction to this terrible news now turned to focus on their lovely daughter. She was totally devastated and completely unconcerned about the curious way her family was looking at her and the questions which lay behind their expressions. This then was the way in which her relationship with Aziz

110

Safwat became known, in a particular set of circumstances that required both patience and forbearance. Ulfat stood up, hugged Siham and took her to her room. Muhammad and Shafiq sat there staring at each other in shocked confusion. Muhammad's face darkened, and he lost his temper.

"You're primarily responsible!" he told his son curtly.

Shafiq was crushed by his father's anger. "It's not my fault!" he replied. He was anxious to be rid of his father's cruel accusations. "It all happened right in front of your eyes!"

"My opinions mean nothing where you're concerned," Muhammad yelled, "your entire generation!"

"Your dream, Papa," pleaded Shafiq, "was that anything could happen outside. But how are we supposed to live outside our own time?"

"I know what people are saying," Muhammad retorted angrily. "I hear it time and again. It's like a cursed plague!"

He gave his son a penetrating stare. "We know that the man had stopped his studies. So how did he manage to insert himself into the midst of the demonstrating students?"

"Maybe he was there as a journalist."

"No, he was there to stir things up as a communist . . . ."

"Could be. I'm not responsible for him . . . ."

"I'm not sorry for him," Muhammad said angrily. "It's myself I'm sorry for . . . ."

Ulfat had washed Siham's face with cologne and shown her more affection than she thought possible. "If only you had controlled yourself!" she said.

"I don't care anymore," was Siham's tearful response.

"Please, I beg you. Get a grip on yourself!"

Poor Siham's heart had been torn apart, and the grief she experienced was fearsome in its cruelty, a looming presence for all eternity, a ghastly wasteland drawing ever closer in order to turn into a never-ending exile. All that remained was a lonely heart beating like the beginning of a melody that has lost its second part forever.

Next morning no one mentioned the 'event' of the day before. The secret kept spreading like sunshine in summer, but everyone looked away and pretended not to see it. Several days passed like this, but then her father decided to break the silence.

"How are you?" he asked his daughter.

She moved her lips, but no sound emerged.

"We all have to suffer," he said with unexpected tenderness. "That's the way of the world. We have to accept God's will without limits or conditions." He patted her hand and went on, "There was a time when I was as happy as you were, with limitless hopes. Then in just a few short hours my world collapsed, and I lost an eye, a leg, and at least half my income. But I was not defeated, nor did my faith in God die. Anyone bolstered by faith will never be brought low. May our God be with you, my daughter!"

In the wake of this paternal peace gesture the curtain of alienation was lifted for a while, but before long the darkness descended once again. The frank truth of the matter was that she now felt a complete stranger within her own family, the kind of feeling that neither affection nor love could cope with. They kept treating her as some 'other' kind of person who no longer existed; in fact, they were her enemies. One wonders whether her father would actually have addressed her in this particular way if he had realized that, by so doing, he was losing her heart and soul. As far as he was concerned, the problem was that she had fallen in love with a young man whose views he totally rejected and who was entirely unsuitable for his daughter. He may even have been quietly happy to have this young man out of the way, hoping all the while that fate would bring his daughter somebody more worthy of her. As the old saying had it, he was in one valley and she in another. For her

112

the only escape was to find some way of getting out of this household where she no longer belonged. Was her revolutionary spirit, the one thing she had really inherited from her beloved, all she had left? So be it! This is how she would remain, stuck between an explosive present and an unknown future that continued to threaten mayhem and scandal.

In the old house Muhammad never said a single word about his daughter's tragedy. At the Friday family gatherings Munira was now the only voice of opposition that kept the conversation moving.

"At last we're living through a period of personal security," Muhammad told her, "after an entire era of fear and terror. Now it's a time for law after chaos."

"Its true barbaric colors have shown themselves clearly," Munira retorted sarcastically, "in the way the demonstrations have been suppressed."

Muhammad's heart shrank. "That was an exception," he said in an unconvincing tone that no one noticed. "The situation demands a certain resolution."

"Everyone keeps talking about the situation. The truth of the matter is that the man doesn't dare go to war."

In his heart of hearts Muhammad agreed with her.

"But why do you want war?" Kawthar asked. "Your two boys will be drafted in two years at the most . . . ."

"I don't want war," Munira said. "What I mean is that they keep using it as an excuse for their barbaric behavior."

"Let's all wish him success!" Saniya chimed in.

"Believe me," said Munira angrily, "he's not going to be content just to purge the negatives of the past. He'll include the positives as well!"

"Say what you like!" said Muhammad with a smile. "The truth of the matter is that there's no comparison between the way things were and the way they are now . . . ."

"What I want to hear," said Kawthar, "is one single piece of news: that the war's over, and Rashad is coming home to get married!"

That comment made Muhammad think about his own family tragedy. He was still amazed that Siham had chosen Aziz Safwat over Rashad. "The only explanation," he told himself, "is my bad luck!"

But indeed there was to be bad luck immeasurably worse than his. It burst into the open like a summer cloud in one of those never-to-be-forgotten moments. A solemn-voiced announcement came over the radio informing the Egyptian people that their armed forces had crossed the Suez Canal.

So, this was war, yet again! Could it really be true that the apparently never-ending lull that had managed to infect the entire country was now being shattered by a nerve-jolting thunderbolt? Had the impossible taken flight, only to dwindle away like some sinister illusion?

"My son!" screamed Kawthar in alarm.

"War again?" Saniya al-Mahdi asked in dismay. "Why do we keep having so many wars, almost as often as prayer times?!"

"I wasn't so scared for nothing!" Kawthar sobbed.

"God is merciful and compassionate," Saniya muttered.

No one in Muhammad's family believed the news, or rather, no one believed the talk of victory. They all still remembered only too well the false information that had been peddled on the radio during the June 1967 War.

"Are we volunteering to commit suicide?" Muhammad asked in despair.

Siham told herself that it was indeed suicide, the kind that might actually provide a little relief from the pain she was still feeling. Indeed a comprehensive defeat was the only way of ridding the country of its reactionary tendencies. Once that had happened, the popular, downtrodden masses might well explode in fury.

As usual, Muhammad and Ulfat turned to the broadcasts from London and America. At first there were conflicting reports, but then the amazing news came through: victory, victory, looming in a magic halo like some stunning miracle that was poised over both imagination and history. A sickly, wan personality vanished, to be replaced by another one bursting with energy and self-confidence. The putrid national sentiment that had been shrouded in the 1967 defeat disappeared, and in its wake was created a new one that could swagger about contentedly as all the dismay, desperation, and oppression associated with the defeat were swept away. Now self, life, and existence were all humming the same tune.

"He's saved Egypt from obliteration; in fact, he's saved the Arabs as a whole . . . ."

Siham was the only one who had hoped Egypt would be defeated. Instead Aziz Safwat had died all over again, the enemy had won, hopes had been dashed, and the future was now shining on the Egyptian reactionary forces that had liberated Sinai. She was still a young woman, lost, rejected, constantly risking exposure.

Munira was fairly happy with things and so was Amin, but in both cases their happiness was marred by feelings of envy and malice.

"How come the great founding figure lost," she asked in despair, "but now the shadow figure has won?" But then she brightened up and went on, "It was Gamal who created and equipped this army!"

Amin grabbed onto this line of thinking like a lifebelt. Even Ali, always negative, found himself temporarily caught up in the euphoria of the moment, but soon enough more urgent problems caused by Mervat's ill health loomed in his life. She was suffering from rheumatism and digestive problems, and her teeth were so decayed that they all had to be extracted. She lost her zest for living and could no longer make love. Old age overtook her all of a sudden, and Ali found himself spending his visits sitting by her bedside, his heart full of sorrow, regret, and disgust.

But then, at the very height of this sense of victory, the frontline was breached. An unexpected and unwelcome surprise, to be sure, and yet one that did nothing to change the basic features of the general picture. Even so, Munira and Amin both managed to view it with a certain malicious glee.

"It's even more ignominious defeat than June 1967 was!" was Siham's incautious remark in full hearing of her parents and brother.

Muhammad frowned. "That's what some of my communist colleagues keep saying," he commented tersely. "Be careful, Siham! You're embarrassing me."

"I'm perfectly free to say what I want," she insisted.

"Yes, you are free," he replied, "but you're also a Muslim woman!"

"Oh no, I'm not!" she told herself, and then said in a louder voice that nobody noticed, "This house is stifling me!"

The fighting stopped, and everyone took a deep breath. The great resurrection had occurred and now there was no turning back. However, the old house in Helwan did not emerge unscathed, or rather not completely. Muhammad was the first to hear the news when one of his friends in the artillery visited him in his office.

"Your nephew Rashad was hit in the fighting on the frontline, but made a miraculous escape!"

From his friend's expression Muhammad could tell that he had not told him everything he knew. He gave his friend a hard, questioning stare.

"He had to have an operation to amputate both his legs."

The expression in Muhammad's one remaining eye showed an intense sorrow.

116

"But we're living in the era of artificial limbs," his friend commented. As he turned to leave, he went on, "Rashad's a hero!"

Muhammad could feel the weight of the responsibility that was now his. He told Munira first, and they both agreed to go to Helwan together. There they found Kawthar in a state of sheer panic, while Saniya seemed quite calm, to such an extent that Muhammad wondered whether she had had some kind of forewarning in a dream.

Munira spoke first. "The war's over," she told Kawthar, "and Rashad is safe, thank God!"

"Really?" Kawthar yelled, at the same time giving them both a doubtful look.

Muhammad started to tell them the truth. "He was hit," he said. "He's a hero, but he's survived."

"My heart never lies to me," said Kawthar.

"He's had a successful operation," Muhammad told her.

Now the truth sank in, and the entire household was overwhelmed with sadness. Everyone was grief-stricken, but even so they still felt a certain gratitude as well. When Rashad finally came home and was carried into the house, tears and joy blended together. From the outset they had put him in a wheelchair. He showed an incredible level of spirit, something that was not mere play-acting but represented a sense of having survived assured destruction, which was in fact the fate of a large number of his colleagues whom he had known for a long time in college, trench, and warfare.

He looked round at the faces of his family who were all staring at him: Saniya, Kawthar, Munira, Muhammad, Shafiq, Siham, Amin, Ali, and Suliman Bahgat.

"All together again!" he said with a laugh.

"This lady doesn't want to give thanks to God!" he said pointing to his mother.

Then he looked over at Siham. "You've been saved from a terrible fate!" he told her, laughing again.

That made her blush. "I'm very proud of you!" she told him.

"May this be an end to wars!" he said passionately.

He was profoundly happy to be home again, a place where he could enjoy both warmth and love. Most of the time he would make light of his injuries, and yet occasionally he allowed his mind to wander, contemplating what was left of his tall frame and remembering how much energy he had had and how he had been able to frequent all those favorite spots of his where he could savor his youth and beauty to the full. With all that in mind, he would nurse some inner sorrows but adamantly refused to surrender to them.

"Live for the moment!" he told himself whenever he had such thoughts. "It's full of limitless opportunities!"

One day his grandmother told him that she was content to conform to God's will. That gave him pause.

"Once you've refused to surrender to the enemy," he told himself as part of his quest for a degree of serenity, "there's no harm in surrendering yourself to fate."

Saniya now decided to fast during the months of Ragab, Shaaban, and Ramadan, in addition to Mondays and Thursdays each week. Kawthar devoted herself to taking care of her son. For his part, Rashad occupied himself in various ways, wheeling his chair out to the veranda when the weather was good, listening to the radio, watching television, and welcoming friends from sporting clubs on designated evenings, all of which helped bring back memories of the evening gatherings that Hamid Burhan had loved so much. On such occasions it was not his mother who dominated the conversation but rather his grandmother. She still had an inexhaustible supply of memories of times past, strange dreams, and intimations of the unseen, not to mention vigorous comments on the situation in today's world.

"How's he going to manage," Kawthar asked her mother one day when they were alone, "when he's left on his own?"

"He'll never be on his own," Saniya replied, relying on her steadfast faith.

For the first time in his life, Rashad found himself enjoying reading. Amazingly, he took to it easily and with a relish. It managed to foster in him a new tendency toward religion. As he consulted an ever-expanding repertoire of religious texts, his interest in the subject gained impetus as day followed day. He was perplexed by any number of issues and found himself drawn toward culture and such interests, all with an enthusiasm that was quite new to him. He even dreamed of writing.

"How little time there is," he told himself one day as he sat there in his wheelchair, "and how short life is!"

"Does a man have to lose half his body," he asked his uncle Muhammad at one of their family gatherings, "in order to discover his own soul?"

His uncle asked him what he meant.

"My invalid status has opened locked doors for me," he replied.

He went on to tell his uncle about his new passion for culture and especially religion. Muhammad was delighted and raised his cane in his right hand.

"Blessed be the one who gives us productive spirits!"

"Sometimes," Rashad went on, "I think of writing things."

"God be praised!" exclaimed Muhammad.

At first it was only a vague yearning, not something formulated according to a particular purpose. But even so, Rashad embarked upon his interest in the Islamic religion with both firm intention and practical bent. He started praying, fasting, and giving alms; he read the Qur'an and al-Bukhari's collection of prophetic traditions. After learning how to deal with what destiny had handed to him, he came to accept it, content to be a participant in the victory, the self-sacrifice, and the heroism. To be sure, he occasionally had nightmares and daydreams in which images of his martyred colleagues would loom, but even that could not ruffle his overall calm.

"Why shouldn't it be possible," he asked himself, "for man to live a happy life on this earth?" And he went on to wonder whether he could find a bride who would be willing to take him as a husband.

This phase in his life coincided with a general shift in direction from east to west, accompanied by the emergence of insistent calls for economic opening up. There was also a veritable explosion of texts that were highly critical of the late president. They appeared in the form of books, newspapers, and journals—a wide-open process that produced a variety of opinions, inimical, supportive, and neutral. Some people were after revenge and simply gloated, while others revived old issues, confessed to past errors, or sought to ingratiate themselves. The entire phenomenon came as a total shock to the older generation, especially people who had come to believe in Nasserism, like Amin, Siham (who in general agreed with it), Ali (who rejected everything), or Shafiq (who by now had taken refuge in a new credo).

"Didn't they all worship him a while ago?"

"Wasn't he the great leader, commander, teacher, and inspirer?"

"What utter hypocrisy! Despicable cowards!"

"It's a generation that needs to be purged!"

"So who are we supposed to believe?!"

"Are we supposed to believe what's being said now?!"

"This isn't a country. It's a public toilet!"

This onslaught was inevitably the topic of lively conversation at the family gathering on Friday. By now Rashad's condition no longer provoked expressions of regret; his circumstances were now generally acknowledged. He had managed to transcend the crisis and move on to something better. For that reason, Muhammad was able to express his delight at the way the Nasserist era was being castigated.

"Let's find out the things we didn't know," he said. "Then everyone who's lost consciousness can wake up."

"But how can we forget the way they put an end to the monarchy?" Munira asked. "Then there's the withdrawal of British forces, agricultural reform, nationalization, Egyptianization of the economy, and Arab national identity . . . ."

"Posterity will grant him one enormous achievement," said Muhammad with a sneer, "the creation of Israeli imperialism!"

"Do you even know what young people are saying?" Munira asked him bitterly.

"You mean, young Nasserists and their atheist allies?" Muhammad retorted. "The majority of young people are perfectly fine. They know exactly what they're doing, just as they know their own Lord."

Rashad joined in the conversation at this point. "Every period has its positives and negatives," he said. "It's up to liberal folks to support the positives and oppose the negatives."

Saniya quoted from the Qur'an, "'Whoever does a single iota of good, God sees it. Whoever does a single iota of evil, God also sees it. God has spoken truly.'"

"No one's ever spoken out against hypocrisy," said Munira voicing her contempt. "That's our real tragedy."

"Gallows are what we've experienced," Muhammad commented angrily, "never hypocrisy . . . ."

"So learn to love this economic infitah!" scoffed Munira.

"What is this 'opening up'?" asked Saniya. "Even Russia's adopted it . . . ."

"In our case, it means inflation and ruin."

At this point Muhammad changed tack. "We're prepared to give it our support," he said, "along with the productivity plan."

"So do I gather that you agree with the values of the cultures that are just waiting to pounce?" Munira asked.

Saniya's heart was full of sorrow. Here they were talking about everything, and yet no one was even saving a good word for the old house. And if that was the case with the house, then what about the family tomb? She looked over at her crippled grandchild, her gaze replete with silent petitions. The family home was very old, the furniture was worn and threadbare, and the garden was dying. Was this an appropriate residence for a national hero?

"Inflation's happening fast," said Rashad. "I can give you an instance from my own experience. A year and a month ago, I offered six thousand pounds for a villa in Maadi. Yesterday I discovered that the owner had turned down an offer of twenty-five thousand pounds!"

"The things people are saying about land prices are hard to believe," Munira commented.

"And downpayments on rentals are absolutely fantastic," Muhammad added.

"Sometimes I think we should repair this house," said Rashad.

"My dear Rashad," Saniya shouted, her heart overflowing with joy, "that's a wonderful idea. A single room in this house is bigger than any of those new villas. And don't forget about the garden. Even though it's been abandoned, it could be turned into a real paradise again . . . ."

Muhammad wondered to himself whether Rashad would regard repairing the house as an act of charity or whether instead he would keep a list of expenses so as not to have to take on all his mother's obligations when the time came—after such a long period—for the house to be passed on to the next generation.

The idea did not appeal to him at all, but he said nothing. Munira and he exchanged meaningful glances which made clear that they were both thinking the same thing.

At this point Rashad surprised everyone. "At some point," he said, "I'm thinking of getting married."

Everyone stared at him, genuinely delighted to hear something they had never anticipated. Kawthar was unable to control her emotions.

"Let's start looking for an appropriate bride," she said.

"Not too fast, mother," he replied. "Everything in good time!"

Inflation now took hold, threatening to become a permanent feature. Arabs from the Gulf started spreading their money around the various quarters of the city like water and air. Prices spiraled out of control; Gulf Arabs proceeded to spend generously, proudly showing off their national identity through petroleum. But, perhaps without really intending to do so, they fanned the winds of inflation. Even Umm Gaber the cook asked for a raise in her salary so she could deal with the soaring prices; her request was granted immediately. Even so, she left the house one day and did not come back. Later they found out that, along with her son who was a carpenter, she had gone to Saudi Arabia to work as a cook at an unbelievable salary. When that happened, life provided yet another warning of hard times to come. To be sure, Saniya had long since confirmed that she was an excellent cook in her own right, but she had now reached an age when it would be impossible for her to undertake the daily chore of cooking, even though she enjoyed the kind of good health that very few of her contemporaries could claim. She still took good care of herself, but, ever since Rashad had come home from the front in the arms of his comrades, she had stopped dying her hair with henna. She allowed the gray to cover her head without hindrance, content to hide it under a gauze and white head scarf. Kawthar now realized that she would have to take over the cooking, even though she was in her mid-fifties. Her liver was still giving her trouble, and she was extremely thin. Her mother and Umm

Sayyid helped her get things ready while they went looking for a cook. Eventually Umm Abduh agreed to work for them part-time for thirty pounds a month. The food budget was consuming a fair amount of money, and the proportion kept increasing day by day, to such an extent that Saniya had to keep her pension for herself out of sheer embarrassment, realizing as she did so that she was now beholden to Kawthar and her son for her very livelihood.

For that very reason Kawthar had occasion to talk to her son when they were alone. "So, you're thinking of refurbishing the house and garden, are you?" she told him. "Be sensible. As you can see, prices keep rising. The house has been around for a long time, but even so we'll only get about a quarter of its value. We have to be careful. Your income is fixed, and it keeps losing value as day follows day . . . ."

"But don't forget that we're living in it," he said in an attempt to postpone any further discussion. "I'm stuck here, and I need a decent atmosphere to live in . . . ."

"As you wish, my son," she sighed, "but please be sensible and cautious . . . ."

Suliman Bahgat surprised everyone by divorcing Munira, claiming as he did so that he was actually liberating her from a situation which had prevented her from doing what she wanted and impaired her happiness without any real compensation. Muhammad was not taken in by the façade; his profession and political activities both enabled him to get to the bottom of things.

"The real issue," he told Munira, "is that both he and his wife work in imports. As we all know, she's the one with the brawn and know-how. She's forced him to divorce you so she can keep the fruits of her labors for herself!"

"That's what I really wanted from the start," was Munira's exasperated comment.

"These days," Muhammad went on, shaking his head sadly, "the Maadi villa is a reception center for wealthy Arabs from the Gulf, a place where you can find a mixture of work and play. Personally I regret very much that both Amin and Ali seem to be drawn to their father."

"Now tell me what our wonderful government has to say about such corruption!" she commented angrily.

"There's no point in moaning about it. Suliman and Zahiya are simply a pair of individuals in a garden full of monkeys. People have gone crazy; they've lost all self-respect. All they do is hover around rich Arabs; those on top whore themselves; those below beg!"

They frowned at each other.

"How are you going to live?" he asked her.

"With each passing month," she replied gloomily, "I ask myself whether we'll be able to maintain our standard of living into the next one."

"I'm the same way. We have children, but there's a distinct risk that they'll plummet to new levels of deprivation. Thank God they've all reached the final hurdle . . . ."

"Yes, and beyond it comes another set of problems," she commented derisively. "What an unlucky, beset generation they all are! Wouldn't it be more appropriate for the Arabs to pull us out of this pit of misery rather than turning us into a haven for beggary and prostitution?"

It was as if Ali was participating in their conversation. Hurling his resentful intentions at existence in general, he cursed his homeland and fellow countrymen and waited for the appropriate moment to abandon it forever. Then came the morning when his mother told him that Mervat Hanem, his uncle Muhammad's mother-in-law, had passed away. Needless to say, she had no inkling of the effect that the news would have on him.

125

"Truth to tell," he told himself as he mourned her passing, "she died months ago."

The woman who had given him a strange kind of love, bestial and out of the ordinary, had managed to provide a cure for his shattered nerves. With her he had experienced a new sense of peace, an all-engulfing egotism, and a rebellious arrogance. Their extraordinary love had presented a challenge to the current poetic clichés; it had certainly rescued him from the clutches of his personal crisis. Yet at the same time it had anchored his recalcitrant vision.

"You did well!" he scoffed. "My brother Amin's the lucky one," he went on with a shrug of his shoulders.

In fact, Amin was very happy. He was in love with a wonderful girl, and she loved him too. But, as he approached the final stage in his education, he could see that his own future would be complicated by a number of problems. However he was delighted when Hind gave her opinion on the topic.

"There's no problem that can't be solved," she said.

"Yes, and we have our love," he went on, suppressing his concerns, "and that's enough . . . ."

Unlike Amin, Hind was not interested in politics or public discourse. She was an excellent student and full of optimism, but her interests were confined to her studies, personal matters, and her own future. At the same time she paid a lot of attention to household chores as though they were an extension of her studies. Her love for Amin was the most cogent factor in her life. As with politics, she was only marginally interested in religion, although it did manage to infiltrate her life—perhaps without her even realizing it—by way of ethics. That is why Amin, who regularly breathed an atmosphere ripe with scandal, came to regard her as a priceless find.

Muhammad's other son, Shafiq, carried on his relationship with Zakiya Muhammadayn until he fell in love with her. Once that happened, he began to have both ideas and worries. At first, he felt a certain degree of alarm, and, as their relationship developed over time, he kept reassessing the situation.

"No one can ever know," he told himself, "where his heart is going to find a resting place!"

The understanding between his father and himself was deep and firmly grounded: father and son, both believers in a single creed. He actually plucked up enough courage to confess to his father that he was in a relationship with Zakiya Muhammadayn and held nothing back about her life. Muhammad listened to his son, trying hard to control his emotions so as to encourage him and sympathize with his situation.

"She's made her mistakes," Shafiq said to bring his confessions to an end, "and has her own justification. The same is true of me."

"No," Muhammad replied shaking his head. "She could have kept her honor intact, and you could have waited . . . ."

Shafiq had anticipated that answer. "What if we both repented?" he asked.

"That is what sinners hope for," Muhammad replied staring anxiously at his son.

Shafiq paused for a few moments. "What I mean is, will you agree to our getting married?"

Muhammad felt fenced in. He was bitterly disappointed and allowed his emotions to take over. "No, that's a bad choice," he said. "There would inevitably be nasty consequences."

"But I thought it would save two erring souls . . . ."

"There's no guarantee of that . . . ." Muhammad commented, and then went on. "What bad luck our family has! We've not even recovered from Siham's bitter experience, but now here you are going down the same slippery path . . . ."

"I thought you'd give my decision your blessing," Shafiq said sadly.

Muhammad spent a considerable amount of time pacing round the valley of his own disappointment. But eventually he collected his thoughts and emotions. "You've heard my opinion on the matter," he sighed, "but, if you insist on taking this step, I'll not object."

Shafiq gave Zakiya the nicest-possible version of the conversation he had had with his father. Zakiya paid close attention to what he was saying. She was by no means as innocent as he was, having been buffeted by life's blows for much of her life. She had a healthy distrust of everyone except herself. As for money, that magic commodity, she had offered herself to it as a sacrificial victim. Now that she was about to graduate, she still had no illusions about what it might bring. After all, life had taught her many more lessons in maturity than her own professors, who had their own uniquely academic methods of horse-trading. Was this young boy really dangling marriage in front of her? Was there any point in it? Why should she have to put up with the contempt that his family would certainly show toward her? In any case, she did not really love him as much as he imagined. These boys were willing to believe any messages coming from a woman's body. On the other hand, she had to admit that he was her most loyal customer and the one she liked the best. She did not like the arrogant way he had offered to marry her or the fact that he had asked her to give up her corrupt way of life, as he put it. So where were all those respectable people supposed to be?

For all those reasons, when he had asked her what she thought of the idea, she had replied that she did not agree.

"Really?" was his shocked reaction.

"Don't get angry," she said. "Just think for a bit, and you'll soon realize that you're not ready for marriage!"

"Me!" he protested.

"Yes, and me too!" she added with a smile.

With that she disappeared from his life like a passing fancy. He almost lost his mind, but, after a good deal of feverish inquiry, he discovered that she too had finally found her own way to the Arab path. In one profitable leap she had managed to move to a fully furnished apartment, taking her long-suffering mother with her. Like her sister before her, she now flew away from the confining cage of daily life and operated on levels far above the aspirations of his particular class.

Muhammad observed his son with a certain alarm and was surprised at the extent to which he kept it all to himself.

"What have you been doing, my son?" he asked Shafiq one day.

"I've come to accept your opinion," he replied tersely.

Muhammad was too experienced to accept that as it stood, but he managed a contented sigh. "May God protect you with His care!" he said.

"But people in my situation need to get married," Shafiq said. "What's to be done?"

Muhammad was at a loss as to how to reply and felt pressured. "Maybe we should be posing that question to the Ministry of Planning," he suggested in exasperation, "or to the economic task force!" He paused for a few moments. "Meanwhile," he muttered, "let's put our trust in Almighty God!"

Shafiq and his cousin Amin both graduated, and Ali, Siham, and Hind Radwan entered their final year. Both Shafiq and Amin were drafted into the army, and Ali found an opportunity to travel abroad as part of the program of seasonal study trips. He did indeed travel, but no one was ever to see him again. He sent a letter to his mother from Germany in which he informed her that he had found a job in a factory; because of his academic training he was considered a skilled worker. Once he had learned enough German, he planned to continue his education. Whatever the case, he would not be returning to Egypt.

Munira read and reread the letter with tears in her eyes. "So now here's another misfortune," she told herself, "to add to my string of bad luck!"

She asked Muhammad to tell Suliman Bahgat about Ali's decision.

Suliman was delighted. "That's the best thing he could have done!" he said. "When I'm on one of my trips abroad, I'll make sure I bump into him so I can offer my blessings for this move he's made . . . ."

"Wouldn't it have been better for him to wait a year until he got his degree?" Muhammad asked.

"He's avoided the draft, and he's right!"

The news was received relatively calmly at the old house. By now they were so inured to bad news that it no longer caused much of a stir.

"Poor Munira," said Saniya, "may God help you!"

"She's been luckier than me!" Kawthar commented.

"Your son deserves to be admired," her mother scolded her, "not pitied!"

She made that comment in spite of the fact that only some of her hopes had come to pass. To be sure, the cracks in the walls had been fixed and the ground floor refinished. The walls were repainted and now gleamed brightly. Mattresses, coverlets, chairs, and books had all been rescued. The gardener had agreed to clean up the garden and plant some jasmine and ivy at the bottom of the walls so the rusty fence could be covered with greenery; he had also agreed to trim the remaining date tree palms. All of which made her very happy, but where did this pathetic patch of garden fit into the dream of the paradise garden that had been promised? What made her feel much more enthusiastic and grateful was the way in which Rashad kept coming up with ways to spend money on the house. He was handing out generous sums as though he was lord of the manor, using his pension only for sundries. How could life have carried on, if it weren't for his ever-generous hand?

Saniya also enjoyed sharing with her grandson not only his daily excursions into books, radio, and television, but also his weekly soirees with visitors. On such occasions she would listen contentedly to his infectious laughter. Here he was, still holding on to his dreams of marriage, writing, and waiting for further light. Rashad was convinced that he had managed to fulfill the dreams of his much-beloved grandmother. He in turn was utterly thrilled to discover that she responded with wholehearted approval to his own dreams.

Unlike his own mother, Saniya encouraged him to start writing. "You've known both war and peace," his grandmother told him. "What more can you ask for?"

She was the only member of the family who, like him, admired both leaders of the Egyptian revolution: the original founder, and his successor.

"Each one of them has his virtues and supporters," she said. "When it comes to their shortcomings, though, all praise to God who alone is perfect!"

"Sometimes I get the impression that you've all lost hope," Rashad told the family gathering one Friday. "My grandmother and I will never give up."

"Inflation's so bad," said Munira bitterly, "that we've forgotten all about the victory we won!" She gave a deep sigh and went on, "And where's Ali?!"

As usual, Muhammad criticized the late president. "All the bad things that have happened to us," he said, "are his fault!" He then turned to the present. "Actually," he went on, "I'm quite satisfied with the current president since he seems like the preparatory phase for the emergence of an Islamic state!"

"When will the crisis ever end?" Rashad asked himself.

Once the visitors had departed, Saniya did what she usually did; namely, went back to the commemorative photograph taken of the family so long ago at the Qanatir Gardens. He pushed his chair over to where she stood and stared at the youthful figures peopling the picture.

"Do you wish you were young again, Grandmother?" he teased her.

"When I look at that photograph," she said distractedly, "I ask myself who could possibly have imagined what would happen!"

Just then he had a brilliant idea. "War isn't the only experience I've had in my life," he said. "Quite apart from that, this picture must have a whole host of amazing stories behind it!"

"Now there's an idea," she muttered.

As she returned to her seat, the sunshine was gradually retreating from the living room. He now recalled the few fleeting comments his grandmother had made about her own ancestry, if only very occasionally. At the time no one in the family had paid any attention, contenting themselves with the fact that they knew about their grandfather who had owned the land and built the house on it. Now Rashad found himself falling under a new magic spell, one that made him want to find out as much as he could about his forebears.

"Grandmother," he told her, "I want you to tell me about our ancestors."

She beamed. "Do you want to write about them as well?" she asked.

"If they deserve it," he replied.

"They deserve that and much more!" she replied with great pride.

He was well aware of how sensitive she was and how she looked at things in her own particular way, so he made a point of hiding his skepticism.

"I'm dying to hear about them," he told her.

She seemed eager to respond and immediately launched into an account of her ancestors. It was almost as though she had been waiting for ages for someone like Rashad to listen to her tales.

"The earliest ancestor I ever heard about," she said, "was called Farag. He came from the far south. He was very strong, and that's how he earned a living. He used to accept gifts, but never grabbed anything by force. So his neighbors both loved and feared him. Both he and his wife were in contact with spirits and the unseen . . . ."

Rashad was astonished, even more so when he saw that his grandmother was being deadly serious. He could not help laughing.

"That means he must have been a highway robber then?" he said.

"If he was," she protested, "no one ever told me about it!"

"But this description of him . . . !"

"If we're going to apply those principles, my dear," she interrupted, "then our esteemed current leaders are all highway robbers too!"

"So you consider him an authority figure, do you?"

"One of their coterie, for sure. Why not?"

He decided to back off so she would continue her story. "You do have a certain point there, Grandmother," he said.

"He reached a hundred years of age," she went on confidently, "but at his very peak he slipped, as it were . . . ."

That made him sit up, but she seemed anxious to move beyond this particular episode.

"Come on, Grandmother," he begged her, "tell me the truth. Otherwise, what's the point?"

She smiled bashfully. "People said," she went on softly, "that he seduced a fifteen-year-old girl."

He managed to suppress a giggle. "Unbelievable!" he whispered.

"It certainly was a 'slip' on his part, but he was a real man!"

"What did the girl's family do?"

"I have no idea. In any case he died shortly after he was mauled by a camel."

So here was his own grandmother, someone who, as far as he was concerned, had always been a paragon of respectability, inner strength, and culture, now revealing herself in an entirely new light, one full of folktale-like stories that are always notoriously difficult to check.

"So," she asked him, "what do you think?"

"He sounds like a great man," he replied, "but I suspect that he won't do our reputation with ordinary folks any good!"

"Haven't you ever encountered things more damaging to one's reputation than a single slip by a hundred-year-old man?"

That made him laugh. "Carry on, Grandmother," he said.

By now she was warming up, and her normally pale cheeks were tinged with red. "The next generation was someone called Ghazal who was generally known by the nickname 'Fleet-foot.' That was because he earned his living by continually moving from one village to another in quest of things to hunt and sell. He rarely stayed at home with his family and never developed any close relationships; it was as though he was always being pursued by someone. That's why he lost the linkage to the unseen world and spirits; he never settled down and enjoyed the comforts of life. To keep himself busy, he used to sing his complaints against the ravages of time. Then came the day when they discovered his corpse floating in a ditch. His killer was never found, and people wondered whether it had been a human being, an animal, or a demon . . . ."

She allowed herself a few moments' silence in order to reflect on the sadness at his passing that showed clearly in her

134

eyes. "I felt so sad about it," she went on, "that I eventually managed to find out how he died . . . ."

"How was that, Grandmother?" Rashad asked.

"In a clear dream," she told him. "I saw a Bedouin highwayman strangling him so he could take his money. Then a wolf came along and ripped his stomach open. A local demon watched the entire thing and then threw the body into the ditch!"

They stared at each other for a while.

"So what do you think?" she eventually asked him.

"Does Ghazal really deserve to be included in the archive as well?" he asked somewhat doubtfully.

"Why not?" she asked in an earnest tone that took him aback. "Has any Egyptian ever been able to achieve a higher status than he did in his own time? He was a striver in life and a martyr in death!"

"What you say is sound common sense," he responded to calm her down.

"Now don't be sarcastic!" she scolded him. "Remember that, in this family of ours, which has seen more than its fair share of escapades and bad luck, I'm the one with the most mature intellect!"

"Rest assured that I'm being perfectly serious. Carry on!"

"Then along came Farag," she went on with a smile. "This was the second Farag, named after his grandfather. After his father's murder he took over the family's responsibilities. Following his mother's advice, he abandoned the itinerant way of life. Instead he chose a profession that was somewhere in the middle: pasturing sheep and selling milk. In that context he managed to enjoy a normal settled existence. He loved both God and women. One day he decided to explode a bomb within the quiet family life he was leading.

"A bomb?"

"Yes! He became a Muslim and adopted the name Muhammad al-Mahdi!"

"How was it our ancestor decided to become a Muslim?" Rashad asked.

"He announced that the Prophet of God—may God bless and preserve him!—had visited him in a dream and proposed that he become a Muslim. He accepted the idea without hesitation. On the other hand, his family was able to confirm that he had fallen in love with a Muslim peasant girl!"

"And what's your opinion on the matter, Grandmother?"

"Thereafter his conduct showed that his decision was sincere. He vowed that his eldest son would attend the Azhar University in Cairo. He was Shaykh Abdallah al-Mahdi, my father and your great-grandfather!"

"Our renowned forefather . . . ."

"Your mother, Kawthar, may well be the only one who remembers him. At first he worked as a teacher, but he could also chant the Qur'an in a lovely voice. Then he purchased some land and devoted himself to cultivating it. He was as renowned for his agricultural skills as he was for his devoutness. When he came down with rheumatism, he moved to Helwan and built this house. It was a little piece of paradise . . . ."

Rashad found himself even more touched by his grandmother's generous nature and delight than by these tales of their ancestors of old. As yet he had not thought about the kind of text he would decide to write, nor indeed about the need (or lack thereof) to include all of them in his account. But his grandmother's enthusiasm in talking about them lent a particular magic to their stories and shed fascinating light on their lives, buried deep in the distant past. All that made him decide to postpone a final decision on format. Instead he started thinking about ways of bringing the garden back to life and thus fulfilling his grandmother's dearest wishes.

"If only I'd thought about buying this house before the economic infitah happened," he told his mother.

Kawthar could read her son's thoughts. "What's past is past," she said. "Remember what I've told you before. Don't overlook the inflation factor; it's not going to die down. The one thing you need to be thinking about is getting married . . . . "

"I'd like to get married here," he said, "even if it involves paying some fee to whoever deserves it . . . ."

"I've an even better idea," said Kawthar with growing interest. "Sell the land and make do with just the building itself. With the money you get for the land you could buy an apartment in one of the condominiums being built in Helwan. Once that is done, you could certainly afford to get married . . . ."

"Leave my grandmother on her own?" he asked.

"No, no," she interrupted. "I would stay with her as long as she was still alive. The important question is this: When are you thinking of getting married?"

"OK," he told her with a laugh, "show me how much you care!"

Kawthar was delighted. "Get all your friends involved in the project as well," she said.

Both Siham and Hind Rashwan had graduated in the same year. Hind was still waiting for a letter of appointment to a position which had still not materialized a whole year later. Siham on the other hand decided to submit a master's thesis, since her obvious excellence led her to aspire for a post as teaching assistant. Shafiq and Amin both finished their required period in the armed forces; Shafiq joined a shipping company as engineer, while Amin took a similar post in a chemical company. Ulfat whispered in Siham's ear that there was a lawyer who specialized in governmental issues who was interested in asking for her hand.

Siham rejected the idea. "I'm not even going to think about that until I've finished my master's degree," she said.

"But . . . ." Ulfat tried to object.

"My big hope is to get a scholarship to study in England."

"But what about your personal life?"

"That's not important!"

Muhammad was well aware of her views on the topic. "You're hard to take!" he said angrily.

"I've a plan, Papa!" she said to calm him down.

"Oh yes," he yelled, "and it's lousy!" Now he was even more annoyed. "In my entire life," he went on, "no one has given me as much pain as you have, apart from Abdel Nasser himself!"

For Siham, this dream of going to England was a last resort, one to which she clung as a matter of principle and as a reflection of her own secret guilt, both being the only surviving relics of her now-dead beloved who had vanished from this world in the twinkling of an eye. Attitudes within her own family were a continual source of worry and concern for her, to such an extent that she was eager to leave her family behind. To tell the truth, she came close to genuinely hating them. She had the strong impression that her father, and Shafiq for that matter, were both keeping a watchful eye on her. Even if that was not entirely true, they certainly did not approve of her lifestyle. Every day that they became more Muslim in their attitudes, the more dangerous they were, and the more alienated she felt. Her mother was of no help whatsoever. She worshiped her father and regarded him as a genuine hero. And, even if she was quite amiable toward her daughter, she too did not support her daughter's attitude toward things. What on earth would happen if Siham's secret were revealed and her lingering sorrows were made public!

Shafiq and his cousin, Amin, shared similar problems.

"What's the use of having a salary?" Shafiq asked.

"None at all," was Amin's simple response.

"I really want to get married."

"I have a fiancée, but I've no idea how we're going to be able to get married!"

"Callgirls have raised their prices on the Arab sexual stock exchange to unbelievable sums!"

"We're hemmed in on all sides."

"Maybe your fiancée will give up hope, and welcome any offer that comes along . . . ."

"She's not that type," Amin replied confidently.

"If I were in your shoes, I'd go ahead and get maried just to give myself some peace of mind. I'd leave the future to look after itself!"

The idea appealed to Amin, but he decided to consider the matter from all sides instead of plunging in head-first like a madman. Having discovered a door that had yet to be opened, he decided to go ahead and knock on it, but to do it secretly. Without even telling his beloved mother, he went out to the villa in Maadi to see his father, Suliman Bahgat. He would occasionally go out there for entirely innocent visits, and it occurred to him that the place was looking more and more elegant and luxurious. As usual, his father greeted him cordially and inquired after the health of his mother, grandmother, and other members of the family. Zahiya was also present, since she would never allow father and son to be alone together. Thus Shafiq could not avoid broaching the subject in her hearing.

"As you know, Papa," he said, "I am engaged. I'd like to get married."

He did not look at Zahiya as he said it, but he was still able to sense that she was having mixed emotions.

"So what's stopping you?" his father asked him somewhat naively.

"You know full well, Papa!" he replied with a nervous chuckle.

Suliman shook his head. "How many times have I told everyone," he said, "that all I own are the walls of this villa?"

"Even if I just asked for a loan?" Shafiq pleaded.

"Grief and sorrow," his father replied sadly. "That's all I have left."

"Listen, chief engineer," said Zahiya, entering the conversation for the first time. "You're rich. You don't need any loan!"

"I beg your pardon?!" he said angrily, turning in her direction.

"Do you have any idea," she asked, "of the real value of your old house in Helwan?" Without waiting for a reply, she went on, "There are a thousand foreign companies who would be eager to buy it for a million pounds. Do you hear me? Don't you people even realize you're worth millions? I'm ready to sell it for you in a single day!"

So Shafiq left the Maadi villa empty-handed. Even so, the thought of those millions kept buzzing around in his head; the world might be created afresh after all. The house belonged to his grandmother, and these days her pension was virtually useless. Selling the house would make her rich, and her children and grandchildren as well. Kawthar, Muhammad, and Munira were all nearly sixty, and life was tough for all of them. His grandmother was in her eighties, and he loved her; or, at least, he didn't hate her. Apart from that, she was in excellent health, much better in fact than either Kawthar or his own mother, Munira. Now a solution was available, one that promised happiness for everyone. At least it would be better than waiting around for her to die before being able to get hold of the key to everyone's rescue plan. He decided to try out this idea on his mother, his uncle Muhammad, and his cousins Shafiq and Siham.

"If everyone forgoes what they're entitled to now," he said, "the inheritance is not liable to death duties. Grandmother will stay wealthy until the very end of her life."

All the family members who were suffering the ravages of inflation thought that it was a fine idea. In fact both Munira and Muhammad had thought of it before, but had decided not to broach the topic out of sympathy for their mother who loved the old house so much and still dreamed of restoring it to its former glory. Why ruin the quiet life of a beloved woman in her eighties? But, faced with the enthusiasm of their children, who were all suffering through really hard times, they found themselves outnumbered.

"You should all realize," said Muhammad, "that neither Munira nor I will be the first to broach this subject."

Siham could not be bothered with the entire matter. "Let them all consume each other!" she thought to herself.

Amin and Shafiq joined the next Friday gathering of the family, a gesture that provoked certain amazement all round.

"It would be nice," Saniya commented, "if once in a while you both remembered that you do have a grandmother!"

Muhammad and Munira felt extremely tense, while both Amin and Shafiq kept waiting for the appropriate point to introduce the subject. Conversation wandered far away from the relevant topic; the principal focus was Rashad's desire to get married. Then politics came to assume its usual central position.

"Our victory has yet to produce any signs of an enduring peace," Rashad commented.

"Quite the contrary," Siham responded without any particular point in mind, "some newspapers are suggesting there may be a fifth war!"

"It's almost as though they're rounds in the soccer championship!" was Kawthar's bitter comment.

The whole conversation turned unusually heated, while their consciences were all burdened by the heavy task that they had all come to perform. For just a moment there was an uncharacteristic silence, during which Amin and Shafiq exchanged glances as a cue for taking the plunge.

It was Amin who breached the anxiety barrier. "We have an idea, Grandmother," he said, "one that needs to be heard."

She gave him an innocent smile.

"Needless to say," Amin went on, "you're well aware of the hardships that people are going through these days, particularly young folks who are looking for a bit of stability in their lives . . . ."

"My heart is with you all," Saniya said affectionately. "God never forgets his servants."

"But there's a solution, Grandmother," Shafiq said.

"I'm delighted to hear it."

"It's all in your hands."

Saniya was astonished. "Mine?" she asked.

"You have a million pounds!" Amin said.

"A million pounds!" she said, looking all around her as she laughed. "All I have is your grandfather's pension, and that goes down every time the sun comes up!"

"As of today," Shafiq said, "this house is worth a full million pounds . . . ."

As though someone had hit her, she fell back in her chair until her back rested against the green-covered sofa.

"This old house!?" she choked.

She looked from Rashad to Muhammad, then to Munira, as though seeking their aid.

"So what are you thinking?" she asked testily.

Muhammad realized at this point that he had to enter the discussion before things got out of hand.

"Mama," he said gently, "forgive them, please. They are all going through really bad times. The only way they know to fend it all off is to gripe . . . ."

"I'm devastated!" she said.

"God forbid!" he said as kindly as possible. "At least give us some time to explore the subject. When all is said and done, you alone have the right to decide whether to accept or refuse. God is my witness that I personally hate this whole idea, but is it right for us to ignore the way our children are suffering?"

"Very well then," she said, obviously exasperated, "I will listen to what you have to say."

"So what precisely is it that the children are proposing?" he asked, invoking his professional skill as a lawyer. "They are saying that foreign companies will purchase the land for unbelievable amounts of money; they believe that we could sell this house for a million pounds. Once that is done, you could buy an apartment or a small villa that suits you and invest the rest of the money in projects that would bring respectable profits. At the same time you could provide your grandchildren with funds that would allow them to establish themselves and fulfill their dreams. That is particularly so in view of the fact that your pension is of little use and the only profit you get from the house is living in it for free. So that's the idea, and we really need to discuss it. No one's going to ask you to make a decision that you don't want to . . . ."

Saniya was so overwhelmed by the whole thing that she did not take in what Muhammad was telling her. The only thing she picked up was that they had all conspired against her in order to make a grab for the house, a place outside of whose walls she could never conceive of living.

"You're all tired of me," she said, "and God does not like such thoughts!"

"Mama," Munira shrieked, "how could you possibly say such a thing? We all love you more than we love ourselves!"

"I had a funny feeling as soon as I saw you all arriving . . . ."

"No, no!" Muhammad chuckled so as to conceal his own bitter feelings, "please forget about such ideas . . . ."

"This is all in fulfillment of a dream I had last night!"

"There must be a good way of interpreting it. It can't be otherwise."

"Very well then" she said firmly, "let's change the subject."

"Grandmother," Shafiq asked, "doesn't it make you unhappy to see us suffering like this?"

"How could it be otherwise?" she replied with great emotion. "You are always with me in my thoughts and dreams, even though you pretend I'm not even here. Where you're concerned, it doesn't make any difference whether you're living in Cairo or Germany . . . ."

"No matter what, you're our beloved grandmother."

She did not respond to that comment. Instead she went on, "According to what we keep reading and hearing, there are lots of opportunities."

"Give us an example," Shafiq asked.

"Gulf countries," she replied. "Not only that, but Amin could start his married life in the apartment in Abbasiya . . . ."

"But any newlyweds want to live in their own place," Amin replied.

"And the Gulf countries don't employ just anyone who asks," commented Amin.

"Well, think about it," she said caustically, "just as long as it's far away from this house."

"Grandmother," Amin said, "it seems that you really don't understand the issue."

"I don't need to," she replied stubbornly. "No one touches this house while I'm still alive!"

She looked straight ahead. "There's just a short span of my life left," she said in a grief-stricken tone reserved for full-scale disasters. "Leave me in peace until God the Merciful decides to call me back . . . ."

"That's the end of the topic," said Munira nervily. "Forgive us, Mama!"

When they had all departed, Saniya closed her eyes wearily. "May God show His mercy and forgiveness!" she muttered to herself.

The next morning, with no particular purpose in mind, she decided to visit the Japanese Garden before autumn came to an end and winter took over. She no longer had the energy she had had earlier in her life. Many memories were gradually disappearing; many dreams would appear and not a few nightmares as well. She would vanish as a woman and take on the form of a banknote enveloped by greed. She slowly walked over to the commemorative photograph on the wall.

"There you are," she whispered, "all the evidence we need of the fact that happiness is a reality, not a dream."

Kawthar spoke to her son. "Start selling the land," she told him. "You've heard and seen enough by now . . . ."

He nodded his head in agreement. "But I'm not going to stint on spending money on the garden," he said.

"I don't understand why," his mother said.

"My grandmother loves me more than all the others," he said gently. "I have to show her the same level of love."

The rest of the family returned to Cairo on the diesel-train, their minds a tissue of conflicting emotions.

"I didn't realize she could be so stubborn!" said Amin.

"She doesn't want to understand," Shafiq said, "or even pretend to."

"I certainly don't intend to live that long . . . ."

"Please remember," Munira said angrily, "that it's our own mother you're talking about!"

Now more personal concerns blended with more public ones. A lot of people were convinced that these issues were all one and the same, although called by different names. The solution involved peace, or was it democracy, or sharia law? The thing that really mattered was that, whatever the solution was to

145

be, it should not be something tried before, something that had grown the whole cluster of bitter fruits they were currently being forced to stomach. So let it be peace, but then why was it so skittish and apparently unattainable? Let it be democracy. Here all kinds of ideas were being discussed and argued about, ranging from political platforms to specific parties. Even the Wafd made its imposing presence felt, like some genie that had smashed its bottle, shaking the earth and resisting all kinds of restrictions that sought to return it to the very same bottle from which it had emerged. Other parties were being formed too; for the first time even the political left had its own authorized party. Every one of these parties advocated the application of sharia law, including the leftists. Muhammad felt that he had never been as close to the achievement of his goals as he was then. Even so, he was not entirely happy.

"Even the communists have their own party," he said, "but we don't."

Voices were raised in opposition, but prices soared still higher and markets were filled with imported consumer and luxury goods. The less well-off started talking about a whole new class of millionaires, as if it were some kind of plague whose symptoms and consequences were only too obvious while the microbes that caused it were invisible to the naked eye.

And then the heavens opened up to rain down on the country a stunning surprise that made everyone forget whatever was bothering them, a kind of fabulous surprise that was beyond the imagination, one with all the hallmarks of wondrous miracles and legends. It was announced that Anwar Sadat was to visit Israel in person! All over the country people gathered around television sets to watch for themselves as human will chose to echo the course of history by changing course irrevocably and without resort to arms. The meeting between former enemies did indeed take place; hands were shaken, and there was an

146

exchange of laughter, speeches, and prayers. From a crack in solid rock sweet water poured forth to flow along a track full of all kinds of pebbles.

Needless to say, this visit was a major topic of conversation the following Friday at the family gathering at the old house in Helwan.

"It's like landing on the moon!" was Rashad's comment.

Both Muhammad and Munira looked unimpressed. At last, the two of them had found something on which they could agree.

"This is a breach that can't be sealed," Muhammad said.

"It's surrender," was Munira's comment, "not peace!"

"What do you want?" asked Kawthar coldly. "Never-ending war?"

Saniya looked serene and happy, even though she always felt a particular love and sympathy for Rashad. "What does Shafiq think?" she asked, looking at Muhammad.

"He's just like me," he replied, "A Muslim through and through."

"And I was a Muslim a quarter of a century before you were," she said. "What about Siham?"

"For the first time ever," he scoffed, "she agrees with us!"

"And Ulfat?"

"I think she's like you, Mama!"

"Does Amin share your views?" she asked, looking at Munira. "Of course he does. At last, they've all agreed about something!" She looked back at Muhammad. "You're some-one who can read people's minds," she said. "So tell me the truth, what are people thinking?"

He tightened his mouth in exasperation. "The people are for peace without common sense!"

"I watched the way they greeted the president when he came back," she said. "My boy, it didn't surprise me at all. They were all renewing their loyalty to him and blessing this step he has taken. They're the ones who've been dying during wartime and starving during the no-war-no-peace. They're simply following their own sound instincts and steering clear of factional intrigues . . . ."

"The real struggle doesn't need to offer any excuses," Muhammad responded stubbornly. "The truth is as clear and bright as the sun itself . . . ."

"Mama," said Munira, "it looks as though we've lost the support of the rest of the Arab world . . . ."

"They've branded us as traitors," said Muhammad, "and they're right."

"What do people have to say about that?" she asked anxiously.

"They're furious at the Arabs," he replied. "They've completely forgotten their history, ancient and modern. Whatever you might say about their mistakes, their support cannot be forgotten . . . ."

"I agree with you on that point. But, as we all know, common sense disappears whenever enemies clash . . . ."

"People have started asking what we have to do with the Arabs. We aren't Arabs, they say. Thus begins another tragic episode in our nation's history, already replete with disasters . . . ."

"Common sense may disappear whenever enemies clash, but it doesn't vanish forever . . . ."

"Now the man has no choice," said Munira contemptuously. "Either he orbits around the United States or we starve to death!"

Even so the old lady remained optimistic. Indeed she started dreaming once again of rebuilding the house and redoing the garden and the family tomb as well.

At this point Rashad informed his uncle Muhammad of his intention to sell land and buy himself an apartment in Helwan. He undertook the task with great efficiency and bought a new apartment in a condominium on al-Amin Street not far from Ibn Hawqal Street. However, his other project, marriage, did not fare so well, even though there were a number of people involved in the search. Every time there was a failure, Kawthar exploded in anger.

"If it weren't for him," she said, "there would be no victory and no peace!"

At long last Munira scored a success for the first time, involving a teacher who was working in her educational department. She was the thirty-year-old widow of a teacher, two years older than Rashad and mother of a ten year-old boy. Her name was Samiha, and she stipulated that her son had to live with her. Kawthar was unenthusiastic as she listened to the woman's description and requirements, but she changed her mind very quickly when she visited Samiha at her father's home in Heliopolis and found her to be both winsome and personable. With a view to Rashad's particular circumstances, she was invited to lunch with Munira at the old house in Helwan, and the couple got to know each other. Rashad was absolutely delighted.

"A gift from God," he declared after Samiha had left.

His grandmother forecast that the marriage would be successful and fruitful. Kawthar and Samiha now set to work, duly helped by Muhammad, to get the new apartment ready. It had already been agreed that Rashad would take on the financial costs involved. At the same time—and also with Muhammad's help—Rashad made arrangements with a gardening contractor to plant trees and bushes in the garden: roses and flowers like jasmine, carnations, narcissus, henna, and roses; and trees, including palms, camphor, cypress, poplar, and acacia. The old lady recovered her spirit of former times, and her head was bursting with new hopes.

"As long as all this is possible," she said, "then anything is . . . ."

Rashad's wedding was a staid and respectable affair, one befitting his condition. It all reminded Siham of the way her own life had been proceeding earlier. For a while she was quite depressed. To compensate, she resolved to work even harder, since her job was the only way she knew of staunching the wound inside her and at the same time opening up doors. As long as she remained in control of her own future, she told herself, she could still hope to find safe shelter somewhere. Beyond that she remained confident of her own unique beauty, even though it could not provide any compensation for the vicissitudes of fate. After all, how could she forget what life had thrown at her aunt Munira? She still felt a strong sense of nostalgia for love and sex as well and was still delighted whenever her male admirers— and how many they were!—flirted with her.

"Somewhere out there," she told herself, "there has to be a suitable man who's broad-minded enough . . . ."

She gradually attached herself to groups of young men and women who shared her political views and thus filled her life with a mixture of companionship and risk.

"Every glass must be drunk to the very dregs!" she thought.

Once Amin had despaired of getting any help from his grandmother (as he had done previously with his own father), he decided to get married anyway. His fiancée's family was delighted by the idea, not to mention Hind Rashwan herself. All of which helped calm his nerves and lessen the burdens that life had thrust upon him. Both he and his cousin Shafiq kept track of the advertisements for jobs in the Gulf countries.

"Now that the Arabs are against us," he asked his cousin, "will that ruin our plans?"

"We have to give it a try," his cousin replied.

Hind Rashwan was doing exactly the same thing.

Munira came up with an idea for Amin. "I could let you have a room in our apartment that you could use as a bedroom," she told him.

"What about the dowry?" he asked.

"At any rate," he said when she did not respond, "people need engineers. We'll find a solution either abroad or in one of the new entrepreneurial companies."

Muhammad assumed that he had found a solution for Shafiq's problems when he found out that a steel merchant (who was one of his colleagues in the Muslim Brotherhood movement) had a daughter of marriageable age.

"Her father's going to take care of everything, even the house," he told his son. "He's agreed to make do with a purely token sum."

Shafiq welcomed the idea with all the enthusiasm of a postulant. But his joy dissipated immediately as soon as he set eyes on the girl. It was not simply that she was not beautiful; she was the spitting image of her father.

"It's as though I'm getting married to the man himself!" he told himself as he recoiled from the whole idea.

"Money, morals, and religion," his father listed for him angrily. "Act like someone who thinks about the inner self!"

With that Shafiq looked at his mother Ulfat. "Oh no," he laughed, "I'm going to be just like you, thinking about both the inner and outer selves!"

"I'm out of ideas!" Muhammad responded with a sigh of anger.

Shafiq was hanging around Talaat Harb Square one day when he came face-to-face with a thrilling sight, his old girlfriend, Zakiya Muhammadayn, coming out of one of the stores and heading toward a blue Chevrolet that was waiting for her. They bumped into each other and stood where they were. They both smiled and shook hands. She invited him to get in beside her, and the car took off. By this time she was no longer the professional student, but had become a full-fledged woman, flaunting herself in a halo of complete self-confidence, clearly wealthy, and sparkling with the panoply of imported grandeur. Now that the flow of Arab wealth had somewhat diminished, her innate disposition may have softened a little. The essence of youth that still lurked in his veins boiled up once again. If only for a short while, all thought of pieties disappeared.

"Why don't you pay me a visit in my new apartment?" she asked, as they headed toward al-Manyal.

As someone living amid the hubbub of Bab al-Luq Station, he was struck by the peace and quiet of her district, wafted by Nile breezes. The décor, mirrors, and objets d'art all fascinated him too, but his amazement reached a kind of acme when he spotted Zakiya's mother—who used to peddle rotten fruit—coming forward to greet him. She was wearing a flashy dress, purple head-veil, and imported slippers, and was carrying a shawl. The sexual urges of old were still raging inside him, and that sent him into a bit of a panic. He had been unable to resist them and had surrendered instantly. He had not touched the glass of cognac; that at least he could do. But, once the claws of this savage beast had withdrawn from his chest, their place was taken by a depression that oozed out like pus.

"Do you still remember the proposal you once made?" she asked him with a laugh.

"Of course," he replied distractedly.

She didn't say anything else. Was she really looking for a husband? With what in mind? He immediately thought of Suliman Bahgat, his aunt's former husband, and Zahiya, and the rumors people had spread. He left Zakiya's apartment with a heavy heart, hoping and praying that he would never have to visit it again.

Like a mirror of the family's various fates, the peace negotiations ground to a halt to such an extent that its supporters became despondent while its opponents gloated. But then at Camp David a difficult birth took place, bringing with it both vistas of pleasure and volcanoes of fury.

The family gathered that Friday as usual, with the exception, that is, of the grandchildren and Rashad who, by this time, had moved to his new apartment on al-Amin Street. It was raining intermittently, and the sky was shrouded in clouds that made the atmosphere in the suburb feel like an ongoing sunset. Work had started on the garden, but it was not progressing as fast as everyone expected because the workers were continually absent abroad. On this particular day there no one was working because it was raining.

Muhammad looked out at the garden which at that point looked as though it had been a target for an air-raid. "It'll be the most beautiful garden in all of Helwan," he said.

"I'm counting the hours and minutes," said Saniya anxiously. "But I keep praying for Rashad from the bottom of my heart . . . ."

"If this is peace," Kawthar commented, "then when do we get prosperity?"

"In fact it's a disaster," Muhammad scoffed. "Islam's the only salvation."

"You're always warning us about disasters," Saniya commented with a smile. "But God can always frustrate people's worst suspicions!"

There was a clap of thunder, and Kawthar shuddered.

"I'm afraid," said Munira, "that there's no going back now."

Saniya looked sadly at the family gathering. They had all aged and grown thin before their time, and that included Muhammad in spite of the determination in his facial expression that reminded her of Hamid Burhan. What had happened to them all? None of them had ever found real happiness, nor had any of their children: Shafiq, Kawthar, Amin, and Ali, they had all suffered the same fate. The only one of them who had managed to settle down was Rashad, but what a horrendous price he had had to pay! Would the house really

153

be rebuilt? Would this mud patch really turn into a beautiful garden? In her imagination it would be a veritable paradise, but in reality it was a piece of land crisscrossed with holes and trenches and surrounded by piles of dirt. When would it ever be finished? When would the plants arrive? When would the rain stop? When would the workers start working regularly?

After they had all had lunch, the rain started pouring down; there was thunder, and wave upon wave of clouds came scudding past.

"We'll have to leave as soon as the rain stops," said Muhammad.

"It would be wonderful if you could all spend the night here," Saniya replied.

"Tell us about your latest dreams!" Muhammad teased her.

"I'm dreaming now," his mother replied listlessly, "and I'm wide awake!"

"Yet another miraculous gift, Mama!" said Munira with a laugh.

Saniya took another sip of her coffee, then called Umm Sayyid and handed her the cup. "Read the cup," she asked her, "and tell me what it says."

"Do you still believe all that stuff, Mama?" Muhammad asked with a laugh.

"It's just like all the other news sources," she replied, "but it's still indispensable!"

The old woman brought the cup close to her weak eyes and spent a few moments staring into it. "You have a long journey in front of you," she said with the same confident tone she had been using for over half a century. "But take a look for yourself" (and she now showed Saniya the cup). "Serenity awaits you . . . ."

There was another thunder clap, and Umm Sayyid almost dropped the cup.

"So tell us, Umm Sayyid," Muhammad asked with a laugh, "when will our troubles be over?"

Saniya looked up and stared first at the sky and then at the garden. She was the one who provided the answer to his question.

"When the thunder stops!" she said.

Afterword

It has sometimes been suggested that this novel by Naguib Mahfouz, in Arabic *al-Baqi min al-zaman sa'a*, published in 1982, is a kind of later version or update of his most renowned earlier work, the so-called *Cairo Trilogy*, namely the three novels *Palace Walk* (1990; *Bayn al-qasrayn*, 1956), *Palace of Desire* (1991; *Qasr al-shawq*, 1957), and *Sugar Street* (1992; *al-Sukkariya*, 1957). While it is certainly the case that there are elements of similarity between the two works, I would nevertheless suggest that, in spite of those similarities (which we will explore below), much water had flowed under the bridge between the Egypt of the 1950s—whether 1956–57 when the *Trilogy* was being published or (more plausibly) Egypt of the pre-revolutionary (pre-1952) period when Mahfouz was conceiving his *Trilogy*, doing the necessary historical research, and writing the enormous work itself—and the Egypt of the late 1970s and early 1980s as depicted and represented in the work translated here. That period of some thirty years had been marked by momentous events and changes, and on both the national, regional, and international levels. Indeed, many of those events and changes are discussed in this novel.

Let me first consider the similarities between the *Trilogy* and the current work. Both seek to place a single Egyptian family into a particular historical context within the broader framework of the development of Egypt and its society in the twentieth century. In the *Trilogy*, the family is that of Abd al-Jawad and its several generations live in the quarters of Old Cairo. The changing locations where the different generations choose to live, beginning with that of the doyen of the family, reflect the political and social changes of the inter-war period—roughly stated, between 1917 and 1944. In the current work, there is also a doyen of the family, Hamid Burhan, and the time period is similarly defined: between the 1930s and late 1970s; in this novel the last political event reflected as part of the family's regular discussions at their Friday luncheon is Anwar Sadat's visit to Jerusalem and the subsequent Camp David Accords. However, from the very first pages of *The Final Hour*, it becomes clear that the 'corporate memory' of this particular family resides with its 'doyenne,' Saniya, Hamid Burhan's wife who, relatively late in the narrative, is questioned by one of her grandchildren, the war hero Rashad, about the pre-history of her family. It is, it would appear, with the early history of her family and its rural origins in the south that we are to locate the authentic ancestry of this much-troubled collection of individuals who have had to face the events of a post-revolutionary Egypt, with its vaunted successes and many trials and tribulations.

The elements of difference that separate the *Trilogy* from *The Final Hour*, apart from the time context of their composition and publication, lie most obviously in the realm of structure. The *Trilogy* is a massive work of more than 1,500 pages, divided into three volumes. As already noted, it deals with a time period of some twenty-six years or so. Not only is each of the three volumes primarily set in a different neighborhood of Old Cairo—giving each volume its title—but also each chapter (following the pattern of traditional models of the European novel) is at pains to place the action not only within a broader historical and social context but also, more exactingly, within precisely defined temporal and spatial frameworks. In one of the several television 'specials' prepared after Mahfouz had won the Nobel Prize in 1988, he even admitted that, in conducting the preliminary research and then composing the text of the *Trilogy* over a five-year period, he had in fact found it necessary to keep a separate file on all the major characters in the narrative so that he could keep track of not only their physical characteristics but also the place and time of their previous involvement in the narrative. What characterizes this particular approach to novel writing (and what has clearly attracted a worldwide readership for the *Trilogy*) is the sheer authenticity with which Mahfouz paints the portrait of a Cairene family in its thoroughly traditional surroundings and in its confrontation with the processes of change. That is, of course, also a feature of many of his other novels from the same period—*Khan al-Khalili*, 2008 (Khan al-Khalili, 1945, for example, and *Midaq Alley*, 1966 (*Zuqaq al-Midaq*, 1947)—but it is in the *Trilogy* that such novelistic features find their richest and most elaborate expression.

In contrast with that approach, the novel translated here is relatively short (190 pages in its original Arabic version), and yet it covers a period almost twice as long. Behind such numerical data lies, needless to say, a series of significant changes in Mahfouz's approach to fiction writing and specifically the modes of depicting time and place—contextualized history in a sense—in novel form. The first thing that will strike the reader of the current work is probably the change in structure. Instead of a three-volume, multi-chaptered work, we are now presented with a single continuous narrative with no chapter breaks. The passage of time and the historical events of the period in question are certainly referred to and discussed by the various members of the novel's family—among themselves and with their friends and acquaintances. Yet the more carefully detailed depictions of specific spaces (rooms, cafés, alleys, and the like) are no longer to be found, nor is the mood of the time or situation illustrated by means of elaborate descriptions of season and weather. To be sure, the primary focus is on a particular house—one in the airy and desirable southern suburb of Helwan, at that. The novel demonstrates the extent to which the various generations of the family are drawn to it and drawn back to it, while younger generations leave it for other locations and uncertain destinies in post-revolutionary Egypt. The organizing device to which Mahfouz resorts in this novel is one that he has used before: a group photograph as a mnemonic device. In a short story entitled "Sura qadima" (An Old Photograph), for example, an Egyptian uses an old school photograph to reflect on his life as he tries to discover what has become of his erstwhile schoolmates. In this novel, the photograph is a family portrait taken during a trip to the Qanatir Park north of Cairo; it hangs on the wall in the "old house," the family home in Helwan. Parents and children of the Burhan family are all there in the photograph. At intervals throughout the course of the novel's narrative and the events that serve as its backdrop, Saniya, the anchor of the family's history and values, turns around in her living room, stares at the photograph on the wall, and wonders how such a seemingly happy group captured by the camera lens so long ago can have suffered so much misfortune in the ensuing years.

Needless to say, the process whereby a writer of fiction like Mahfouz moves from the techniques of the *Trilogy* to those of *The Final Hour* is one that can be traced through a number of intervening works. The move to a greater economy in description and an increased reliance on the dramatic possibilities of dialogue was already evident in Mahfouz's most controversial work, *Children of Gebelawi* (1986); *Children of the Alley* (1996) which first appeared as *Awlad haratina* (original articles, 1959; in unauthorized book form, 1967) and was to be continued and developed in the series of novels that Mahfouz published in the 1960s. However, the June 1967 War and its aftermath were to be a watershed for Mahfouz and almost every writer throughout the Arab world. As in the post-revolution period (1952–56), so in the immediate post-1967 period (1967–72) Mahfouz published no novels, somewhat remarkable in view of the fact that earlier in the 1960s he had been publishing one a year. What he did do was publish a series of highly symbolic short stories in which the themes of alienation and civic responsibility (or lack thereof) were framed in atmospheres of ever-impending menace and gloom. In the grim and often recriminatory aftermath of Nasser's death in 1970—yet another event mentioned in the current novel—Mahfouz penned what is probably his angriest novel, *Karnak Café* (2007; *al-Karnak*, 1974), a gruesome retrospect on the darkest days of the 1960s and the all-pervasive presence of the secret police. The fact that Mahfouz notes at the end of that text that he completed it in 1971 but it was not published until 1974 tells its own story. *Karnak Café* was followed by another work, similarly retrospective but, at the same time a sign perhaps of things to come: *Mirrors* (1977, 1999; *al-Maraya*, 1972). Here Mahfouz, who has by now retired from his position as a cultural bureaucrat and become a weekly columnist for the Cairo daily *al-Ahram*, shows that the experimental urge that marked his works of the 1960s has not deserted him. The filing instincts of the bureaucrat, mentioned earlier in connection with preparations to compose the *Trilogy*, are now combined with the creative talents of a writer who never wishes to stay in the same place: we are presented with a sequence of fifty-four vignettes portraying Egyptian characters with whom the 'narrator' has come into contact. The vignettes are arranged in alphabetical order, and many of them are cross-referenced, a remarkable compositional feat by any standards. The word 'narrator' above is placed in quotation marks because, as several cognoscenti of the Egyptian cultural scene have pointed out, many, if not most, of the 'characters' portrayed in these vignettes are clearly identifiable as actual persons. This same experiment in alphabetical organization is to be repeated in the equally accomplished *Morning and Evening Talk* (2007; *Hadith al-sabah wa-l-masa'*, 1987) which traces the interconnected histories

160

of several Egyptian families from the time of Napoleon's invasion of Egypt in 1798 into the twentieth century.

The Final Hour, then, belongs to a period in Mahfouz's career during which he is continuing to comment on the life and circumstances of his homeland, but is doing so through increasingly interesting experiments in structure and style. Thus we have, for example, a modern replica of the traditional multi-generational saga in *The Harafish* (1994; *Malhamat al-harafish* 1977), characters from *A Thousand and One Nights* in *Arabian Nights and Days* (1995; *Layali alf layla*, 1981), and a travelogue in quest of a society where religion, secularism, and morality may co-exist in *The Journey of Ibn Fattouma* (1992; *Rihlat Ibn Fattuma*, 1983), the very title of which invokes the earlier travelogue of Ibn Battuta (d. 1368). And, if the retrospective aspect is already prominent in the current novel, it becomes even more so—verging on the wistful—in later works, such as *Qushtumur* (1988 [name of a café]). Beyond that, the terrible attack on Mahfouz in October 1994 may have put an effective end to his writing career in the literal sense, but he continued to share his creativity and ideas with his readers, dictating materials in either article form or as contributions to fiction. His final works, including *Echoes of an Autobiography* (1997; *Asda' al-sira al-dhatiyya*, 1994); and *The Dreams* (2004) or *Dreams of Departure* (2007; *Ahlam fatrat al-naqaha*, 2004), take as their focus the recollection of the past and contemplation of the deeper concerns of humanity and express them through an even greater use of economy and allusion.

Like other families that Mahfouz has created for his readers—and indeed, like the Abd al-Jawad family of the *Trilogy*, the members of Hamid Burhan's family, and especially his children and grandchildren, find themselves pulled in different political directions. Hamid Burhan, for example, is a lifelong supporter of the Wafd Party in the pre-revolutionary period and, like his creator, a fervent admirer of the party's founder and figurehead,

Saad Zaghlul. His son, Muhammad, on the other hand, is increasingly drawn toward the mission of the Muslim Brotherhood, an affiliation that leads to his arrest, imprisonment, and brutal torture. He emerges a cripple with only one functioning eye, and yet, throughout the novel, his commitment to Islamic traditions and his diehard opposition to the secularist policies of the new regime and its leaders are unswerving. Almost at the opposite end of the political spectrum, Siham, Muhammad's own daughter, acknowledged as being as beautiful and talented as her aunt, Munira, falls in love with an ardent socialist, Aziz Safwat, and finds herself increasingly alienated from her father, her family, and everything that it stands for. It is not without reason that Saniya keeps staring at the photograph on the wall and wondering what has become of her family and Egypt in general.

It is, of course, part of Mahfouz's genius that so many aspects of Egyptian history and social life during a period of enormous change and upheaval can have been encapsulated into such a relatively short work. Experiments with party-based democracy, the impact of the Second World War and its aftermath, the July 1952 Revolution, the emergence and triumphs of Gamal Abdel Nasser, the debacle of June 1967, the early years of Sadat's presidency and the impact of *infitah* (economic opening up), the arrival of many inhabitants of the Arabian Gulf for either business or pleasure (or both) and, as already noted, the Camp David Accords, all these are alluded to in the text—and a glossary with supplementary information is provided for those readers who may find the allusions too illusive. As the younger members of the family grow up and are trained within the context of the new post-revolutionary educational system, they almost inevitably find themselves reflecting new loyalties and political configurations and confronting and challenging older ones. Whether it is at Hamid Burhan's evening gatherings with his colleagues earlier in the novel or at the Friday lunches at which the younger generations meet at their mother's (or grandmother's) house in Helwan, the momentous changes that are presented by these national and international developments are discussed at length and often with radical disagreement—much to Saniya's discomfort. Between tradition and modernity, secular values and religious beliefs, increasing poverty and wealth in the context of gross inflation, and the changing roles of men and women within the family and society at large, all these issues are exemplified and explored in the different paths that the younger members of Saniya's family pursue in their public and private lives.

In this novel then, Naguib Mahfouz's carefully crafted gift for succinct and authentic fictionalization of large topics in maximally economical and richly allusive form is wonderfully illustrated. It thus constitutes another, albeit very different, account from his pen of the paths taken by modern society and politics within his homeland, Egypt, during the twentieth century.

Glossary

1919 Revolution in 1918, an Egyptian delegation (Arabic *wafd*) demanded the right to travel to London to discuss its conditions for independence. When their stipulations were denied and the leaders (including Saad Zaghlul, the figurehead of the movement) were exiled to Malta by the British authorities, a widespread revolt broke out which became known as the 1919 Revolution.

1923 Constitution announced in April 1923, the Egyptian Constitution was an attempt to resolve a political crisis that had its origins in the expulsion of Saad Zaghlul by the British forces and the continuing manipulation of power by both the British authorities and the king. Continuing opposition to the constitution focused on the wide powers that the king retained, not least to appoint the prime minister and dissolve parliament.

1967 War the June 1967 War (known in Arabic as *al-naksa* [the setback]) was a devastating blow to Egypt and the entire Arab world. In territorial terms, it led to the loss of Sinai (later returned), the Golan Heights, Jerusalem, and much of the West Bank of Jordan.

Agricultural Reform Laws in Egypt, as elsewhere in the Middle East region, one of the first measures taken by the revolutionary authorities was to enact the Agricultural Reform Law (1955) that redistributed land ownership by taking large tracts of property away from the landed gentry and reassigning them to peasants.

The Anglo-Egyptian Treaty of 1936 this treaty, giving Britain the right to retain troops in Egypt to 'protect' the Suez

Canal, aroused opposition in Egypt and considerable anti-Wafdist sentiment. Mustafa al-Nahhas was one of the signatories to the treaty, but, while prime minister again in 1951, he denounced it.

Anwar Sadat's visit to Israel in 1977 Egyptian President Anwar Sadat broke the longtime taboo against contacts with Israel by visiting Jerusalem and addressing the Knesset. This was the beginning of a process that led to the Camp David Accords between Egypt and Israel.

Archaeology [Egyptian] Museum while an "Egyptian Museum" to house the country's huge collection of artifacts was founded as early as 1835, the current building on Tahrir Square in central Cairo received the collection in 1902 from an earlier building on the opposite bank of the River Nile in Giza.

Basmallah the phrase "In the name of God, the Compassionate, the Merciful," regularly invoked by Muslims when initiating an activity of any kind.

Cairo fires in January 1952 several prominent buildings in central Cairo (including the old Shepheard Hotel) were torched in reaction to the death of a number of Egyptian policemen at the hands of British forces near the Suez Canal. The event is generally regarded as a prelude to the Revolution that brought the Free Officers to power in July of the same year.

Camp David Accords the peace agreement fostered by American President Jimmy Carter and co-signed by Anwar Sadat, president of Egypt, and Menachem Begin, prime minister of Israel.

Crossing the Suez Canal called *al-'ubur* in Arabic, the attack on the Bar Lev Line in October 1973 was the beginning of a conflict with Israeli forces that was declared by the French scholar Jacques Berque to be a "psychological victory" for Egypt, even though Egyptian forces were eventually driven back to the Egyptian side of the Canal.

February 24, 1942 incident as part of the tensions between Egypt and the British authorities that existed during the Second World War, the British ambassador in Cairo demanded in February 1942 that the young King Faruq appoint Mustafa al-Nahhas as prime minister. When the condition was refused, British tanks and troops were sent on February 24th to surround the Royal Palace in Abdin (central Cairo). Under duress, the king was forced to give way and appoint al-Nahhas.

Infitah the Arabic term (meaning economic opening up) used to describe the decision by President Anwar Sadat in the 1970s to release the Egyptian economy from the tight controls under which it had operated for a decade or more and to encourage foreign investment in the country.

Japanese Garden, Helwan these gardens in the town of Helwan, to the South of Cairo (recently [2009] restored), have long been recognized as a quiet haven from the bustle of the enormous city of Cairo to the north. The gardens contain a number of Japanese structures and monuments, but are best known for their open spaces and tree-lined walks.

July revolution the event in July 1952 that ousted King Faruq and brought to power the group of "Free Officers," initially led by General Muhammad Naguib. Subsequently, Gamal Abdel Nasser was appointed leader of the group and became president of Egypt until his death in 1970.

Mahmud al-Nuqrashi (1888–1948) leader of the so-called Saadist offshoot of the Wafd party, who was twice prime minister of Egypt in the 1940s. He was assassinated by a member of the Muslim Brotherhood in 1948.

Muslim Brotherhood founded by Hasan al-Banna (1906–49) in 1928, the *Ikhwan al-muslimun* rapidly became a powerful movement of popular Islam, especially in Egypt and in other countries of the region as well. It has remained a major political force until the present day. Frequently persecuted by a succession of secular government authorities, the movement still maintains a vigorous presence in social and political life in Egypt, not least through its role in various spheres of social work.

Mustafa al-Nahhas (1879–1965) the major leader of the Wafd Party following the death of Saad Zaghlul in 1927. During the extremely fractious period in Egyptian political life between the two World Wars, al-Nahhas was prime minister on several occasions, the last time being until January 1952. As Mahfouz portrays in this novel, Nahhas's funeral in 1965 was an occasion when, much to the displeasure of the Egyptian regime, many frustrations at the course of the 1952 Revolution burst into the open in a huge public demonstration of nostalgia for a parliamentary past that had been abolished.

Palestine conflict in 1948 known in Arabic as *al-nakba* (the disaster), the conflict broke out after the approval of the partition of Palestine endorsed by the United Nations in 1947, the subsequent withdrawal of British forces who had supervised the 'Protectorate' since the conclusion of the First World War, and the declaration of the establishment of the State of Israel.

Qanatir Park a popular venue for excursions to the north of Cairo, alongside a barrage on the River Nile. Construction of the barrage began in the nineteenth century and was completed in 1910.

Saad Zaghlul (1859–1927) the leader of the Wafd Party, a prominent national figure in Egyptian nationalism, and Naguib Mahfouz's personal hero.

Singers (Umm Kulthum [1900–75], Muhammad Abdel Wahhab [1907–91], and Abdel Halim Hafiz [1929–77]) these are three of the most famous Egyptian singers during the twentieth century. From his youth, Mahfouz was very interested in singing, and Umm Kulthum was a special favorite of his and of people throughout the Arab world. Abdel Wahhab belongs to an older generation than Hafiz but outlived him. All three singers commanded enormous public audiences during their singing careers.

Socialist Laws in 1961, these laws were passed nationalizing large segments of the Egyptian economy, including banks, publication, and the press. A single party, the Arab Socialist Union (ASU), was established and remained the sole arena of political activity until the June War of 1967 and its aftermath.

Suez 1956 following the Czech Arms Deal of 1955, President Nasser nationalized the Suez Canal, which resulted in the so-called Tripartite Invasion (involving Britain, France, and Israel) in 1956. The United States refused to condone the operation, the invading forces were withdrawn, and Nasser became a hugely popular figure throughout the Arab world and beyond.

Umar ibn al-Khattab (c. 586–644) the second Islamic Caliph and son-in-law of Muhammad the Prophet, renowned as a lawgiver and often referred to as al-Farouk (the arbiter).

United Arab Republic the growing popularity of President Nasser throughout the Arab world in the wake of the nationalization of the Suez Canal in 1956 led to the unification of Egypt and Syria as the United Arab Republic between 1958 and 1961, with Nasser as its president.

Wafd Party founded as a result of Saad Zaghlul's demand to petition the British government for independence, this Egyptian political movement played a major role in the interwar period in Egypt. As several of Mahfouz's fictional works clearly illustrate, Zaghlul was to remain a major hero of the author throughout his life. The Wafdist narrator of Mahfouz's novel *Miramar*, Amir Wagdi, for example, seems to be expressing his creator's nostalgic feelings for the days of parliamentary rule and Wafdist control of the country in the era before the 1952 revolution.

Yemen Revolution in 1962 a revolution in what was then known as "Northern Yemen" (later joined to "Southern Yemen") overthrew the ruler of the kingdom of Yemen and installed a Yemen Arab Republic under the leadership of Abdullah al-Sallal. President Nasser sent a large force of Egyptian troops to Yemen to support the revolution, but the conflict, which dragged on for many years and was only resolved by a peace agreement in 1970, proved to be increasingly unpopular in Egypt.

Modern Arabic Literature
from the American University in Cairo Press

Edwar al-Kharrat *Rama and the Dragon* • *Stones of Bobello*
Betool Khedairi *Absent*
Mohammed Khudayyir *Basrayatha*
Ibrahim al-Koni *Anubis* • *Gold Dust* • *The Puppet* • *The Seven Veils of Seth*
Naguib Mahfouz *Adrift on the Nile* • *Akhenaten: Dweller in Truth*
Arabian Nights and Days • *Autumn Quail* • *Before the Throne* • *The Beggar*
The Beginning and the End • *Cairo Modern*
The Cairo Trilogy: Palace Walk, Palace of Desire, Sugar Street
Children of the Alley • *The Coffeehouse* • *The Day the Leader Was Killed*
The Dreams • *Dreams of Departure* • *Echoes of an Autobiography*
The Essential Naguib Mahfouz • *The Final Hour* • *The Harafish*
In the Time of Love • *The Journey of Ibn Fattouma* • *Karnak Café*
Khan al-Khalili • *Khufu's Wisdom* • *Life's Wisdom* • *Midaq Alley*
The Mirage • *Miramar* • *Mirrors* • *Morning and Evening Talk*
Naguib Mahfouz at Sidi Gaber • *Respected Sir* • *Rhadopis of Nubia*
The Search • *The Seventh Heaven* • *Thebes at War*
The Thief and the Dogs • *The Time and the Place*
Voices from the Other World • *Wedding Song*
Mohamed Makhzangi *Memories of a Meltdown*
Alia Mamdouh *The Loved Ones* • *Naphtalene*
Selim Matar *The Woman of the Flask*
Ibrahim al-Mazini *Ten Again*
Yousef Al-Mohaimeed *Munira's Bottle* • *Wolves of the Crescent Moon*
Ahlam Mosteghanemi *Chaos of the Senses* • *Memory in the Flesh*
Shakir Mustafa *Contemporary Iraqi Fiction: An Anthology*
Mohamed Mustagab *Tales from Dayrut*
Buthaina Al Nasiri *Final Night*
Ibrahim Nasrallah *Inside the Night*
Haggag Hassan Oddoul *Nights of Musk*
Mohamed Mansi Qandil *Moon over Samarqand*
Abd al-Hakim Qasim *Rites of Assent*
Somaya Ramadan *Leaves of Narcissus*
Mekkawi Said *Cairo Swan Song*
Ghada Samman *The Night of the First Billion*
Mahdi Issa al-Saqr *East Winds, West Winds*
Rafik Schami *The Calligrapher's Secret* • *Damascus Nights*
The Dark Side of Love
Habib Selmi *The Scents of Marie-Claire*
Khairy Shalaby *The Lodging House*
The Time-Travels of the Man Who Sold Pickles and Sweets
Miral al-Tahawy *Blue Aubergine* • *Gazelle Tracks* • *The Tent*
Bahaa Taher *As Doha Said* • *Love in Exile*
Fuad al-Takarli *The Long Way Back*
Zakaria Tamer *The Hedgehog*
M.M. Tawfik *Murder in the Tower of Happiness*
Mahmoud Al-Wardani *Heads Ripe for Plucking*
Amina Zaydan *Red Wine*
Latifa al-Zayyat *The Open Door*